HONEST LOVE

HONEST LOVE

ESKAY KABBA

4 Horsemen
Publications, Inc.

Honest Love
Hidden Love Series Book 5
Copyright © 2023 Eskay Kabba. All rights reserved.

4 Horsemen Publications, Inc.
1497 Main St. Suite 169
Dunedin, FL 34698
4horsemenpublications.com
info@4horsemenpublications.com

Cover and Typesetting by Autumn Skye
Edited by Blair Parke

Library of Congress Control Number: 2022952425

Paperback ISBN-13: 978-1-64450-824-4
Audiobook ISBN-13: 978-1-64450-825-1
Ebook ISBN-13: 978-1-64450-823-7

DEDICATION

To my mother, the strongest woman I know.

This book contains scenes of racism, volience, and homophobic slurs. Please consider your triggers before reading.

TABLE OF CONTENTS

CHAPTER 1

WELL THEN DON'T BE AN ASSHOLE

Connor

Afia plopped into Jamel's empty seat next to me. "Ugh, I need a break." I took off my headphones to hear her better. "Tyriq is crying a lot because he hates the plane, and the girls are just really loud, and I have a headache."

I smiled at my best friend. "So, you left your kids alone on the other side of the plane?"

"Noooo," she emphasized. "Jamel came over with Zee and Vee and is keeping them company, and Tyrell is walking Lil Ty up and down the plane, trying to soothe him. But the only thing that soothes him are boobs." I watched her massage both softly. "I'm a little sore."

"Going to stop breastfeeding early?" I asked.

She sighed. "No, not until he's ready."

"He's a boy, he's never going to be ready," I said with a laugh.

She smiled and turned to me. "You're good? We haven't really spoken since we were all together dealing with Winter's … situation. Aruba was good?"

I nodded while I was smiling hard on the inside. "Aruba was great. Just what we needed to feel connected again."

"Hmmm. Sounds like there was a whole lot of fucking happening," she said and giggled.

"A lot," I confirmed, then I started giggling.

She put her head on my shoulder and took my hand. "I just realized it's the first time we're on a plane together."

"I think you're right, Lovie."

The whole Jones clan was headed to Miami for Thanksgiving to spend it with Major Wendel Jones and Mama Denita. When they made the decision to move to Miami two years ago after another heart attack scare from The Major, it was the first time I ever really saw Jamel outright cry. The Major lined all his sons up in his office, myself included, and told us that we were amazing young men and going to be fine without him. Then he individually told us that he was proud of us, loved each of us, and why: he loved that Lavell was always the smartest man in the room; he loved that Donell was a great dad and a role model for Black men; he loved Tyrell's dedication to his family and the family business; he loved Jamel's innate ability to lead and mentor everyone around him; and he loved my fierce loyalty to Jamel, the whole Jones family, and veterans everywhere. Usually when Jamel cries, he just lets a few tears fall from his eyes, but he was ugly crying with the rest of us as his father spoke. It was hard to let him go, but we knew we had to.

We hadn't seen them since they came back to Rhode Island last year for my and Jamel's wedding. It was nice that our parents rented a beach house for all of us to be together: Lavell's family, Ty's family, Donny's family, and Jamel and I. Donny and Vanessa were coming with DJ, flying down on Thursday and leaving Saturday, while we were there from Wednesday to Sunday. I planned to spend some individual time with the old man, see how he was doing, and catch him up with what was going on with work and vet stuff, as well as get hugs from my mother-in-law.

I was in the best stage of my life: in my mid-thirties, married to an amazing man who just celebrated ten years of love and commitment with me; my best friend of twenty years was my sister-in-law; and I owned my own home, had two beautiful dogs, and a stable career as CEO of my organization, Vinnie's Vet Buddies. I was coming into the holiday more accepting of myself, my sexual identity, and who I was as a person than ever before. I had good friends and a family, the Jones family. I didn't tell Jamel yet, but I secretly got my driver's license changed after we came back from Aruba, hyphenating my last name to McIntyre-Jones. I should have done it a long time ago; Jamel's family had been my family since I met my husband back in 2009.

But more importantly, I wanted to show Jamel, show the world, that I was proud to be his husband. Jamel Jones has stood by me through it all: me being in the closet and my whoring ways when we met; trying to ghost him, more than once, because I was afraid of my feelings; him finding out about the physical abuse I experienced as a child all the way into my twenties; me almost going to prison for shooting my father, Owen McIntyre; and him very recently finding out about my suicide attempt fifteen years ago. If there were medals given out for the most patient, understanding, accepting, forgiving, and loving husband in the world, Jamel would have the biggest one. I absolutely knew I didn't deserve him, even now. I could be an asshole sometimes; it was kinda my default. But I was grateful that he felt me worthy enough to take a chance on me and stay with me, throughout it all.

Lovie and I were talking softly with each other when Tyrell, her husband, came up to us, holding his son. "He needs you, Fifi."

She sighed as she looked up at him. I began to stand up and said, "I got him."

But Ty held the toddler back from me and said, "He needs Afia."

I couldn't help it. "Afia needs a break. That's why she came all the way over here, to get a break."

Afia began to say, "It's fine, Connor—"

But Tyrell said harshly, "Don't tell me about my wife, Connor." He stepped back and commanded her, "Let's go."

She glared at him like she wanted to curse him out, but we all could tell others around us on the plane were listening. She stood up, took Tyrek from her husband, and walked down the aisle. I realized I was still partially standing, as much as the overhead compartment would let me. It must have shown all over my face how pissed off I was at the way he talked to her because Ty sneered at me as they left.

"*What?* Something you wanna say?"

He was testing me, and I wasn't going to take the bait. Ty and I did not have the best relationship and every once in a while, he tried to provoke me. This was obviously one of those times.

I slowly sat back down. "Just make sure she gets breaks this weekend."

He leaned in and said, "Don't tell me how to take care of my wife, Connor. She's *mine*, not yours." He went back to their seats further up and on the other side of the plane.

I sat there and stared at the screen in front of me, trying to calm myself down. Jamel appeared and sat down in his seat. He looked over at me and said, "What's wrong?"

I said, without looking at him, "One day, your brother is going to take a swing at me."

He sighed. "Connor, I asked you—"

"I know what you asked me," I interrupted him. "And I've been the mature one, the one to back down, the one to let it go. But one day, he's going to take a swing at me." I turned to look him in the eye. "And I'm going to swing back."

We held eye contact. He looked away first.

The rental home was an eight-bedroom waterfront in north Miami Beach, ten minutes away from the strip. We rented two cars, one for us and Lavell's family, and the other with Ty's family. The Major met us out front, looking healthy and strong. Tykeya, Tenille, Ty's girls, and Xiomara and Vienna, Lavell's girls, all ran for their grandfather and made him tumble over onto the ground. It was nice to see him smiling and hugging them, since The Major is known for not being an emotional or affectionate man.

Mama Denita screamed from somewhere inside the house, "Where are my grandbabies!?" The children let their grandfather go and ran inside to find her.

The Major stood up, put back on his straw hat, and dusted off his blue silk shirt and white linen pants to come up to us as we were uploading the car. Jamel approached him first, saying, "Major *who*? I'm gonna start calling you Don Papi!"

His father surprisingly let out a big smile at Jamel's teasing. He took his hand and shook it, then pulled him into a half hug, also surprisingly.

"You been drinking, Pop?" Ty asked, as he also gave his father a half hug.

"Have you?" his father asked him back with an eyebrow raised. Ty didn't answer, just slowly let him go.

The Major turned to me and smiled widely. "Hey, Connor."

"Hey, Pop," I greeted him. He attempted to give me a half hug, but I threw my arms around him and grasped him tightly. He laughed and pretended to punch me on the side. I let him go and pretended to fall out, making him laugh some more. The man and I had a pretty good relationship, and ever since I put a bullet in Owen, I considered The Major my father.

He turned to Lavell and gave him a full hug. "You look good, Major," Kendra said kindly and wrapped her arm around him. Afia did the same, and they walked into the house together.

Jamel and I picked a room that overlooked the pool area. I leaned over the rail and watched Afia and Kendra get their kids dressed in bathing suits from the balcony. The girls happily jumped into the two-and-a-half foot section and waded. Afia took her time putting floaters on Lil Ty and casually slid in with him tightly grasping her neck. Tyrell came over and said a few words to her, then took his son. They kissed, and she swam over to the deep end while Ty sat on the edge, playing with their son and keeping an eye on their daughters. The Major came out with Lavell, and they sat on the side under one of the umbrellas and talked privately. Every one of his sons was going to want to have one-on-one time with him. I made a note in my head to find a way to catch him, too.

I heard Jamel say, "Come inside, baby."

I had left him in the room to organize our clothes in the dressers, but when I walked back in, he was under the sheet, and I could tell he was naked. I smiled at him and closed the balcony door tightly.

"We're right over the pool area," I told him, as I took off my shirt and walked to him. "Everyone is out there."

He pulled me by the top of my jeans roughly onto the bed and said, "Then you better be quiet."

He kissed me and bit my bottom lip, and I liked it. I kissed him back with the same intensity. Jamel made his way down, kissing my skin along the way. But he bit my nipple hard, making me cry out. He looked up and shook his head, reminding me to be quiet, then leaned down and licked my nipple to soothe me. He moved over to the next nipple and bit me again. I grinded my teeth together to keep from yelling, but he made it difficult, holding it in his teeth a little longer than the first one. I grabbed onto the sheet tightly, whimpering until he began to cool the pain down with his warm tongue.

Jamel looked up at me and smiled. "You like that?" he asked softly. All I could do was nod. My cock was completely stiff, and I was panting below him.

He unbuckled my jeans and slid them off but not my underwear, not yet. Instead, he made his way down, nibbling some more. He licked the inside of my thigh, then bit me again. I didn't expect that, and I almost cried out again as my back arched off the bed. He chuckled below me.

"Since when did you become a biter?" I asked breathlessly.

He moved up over me and said, "I guess I learned a few things in Aruba."

I did a small intake of breath, and he pressed his lips down on me before I could respond. We kissed passionately and pushed our groins together as I held onto his muscled ass. He bit the space between my neck and shoulder like he normally did, but with a lot more pressure. He dug his pelvic bone deeper into my midsection, sliding against my genitals. His entire weight was on me, his teeth clamped onto my neck like a vampire. I had nowhere to move, no willpower, so I surrendered it all to him. My cock released right into my black thigh high briefs, and I moaned out his name, "Jameeeeel."

He stopped moving and looked up at me, then he let out a sly smile. He sat all the way up onto his legs and motioned with his fingers for me to come to him. I did, crawling on my hands and knees to his waiting cock. I engulfed him, came up and engulfed him again. The third time he stopped me from coming up, holding my head into place, and thrusted upward. Slowly at first, then picking up speed.

This was new. Jamel likes to make love to me. Even when we are hard-core fucking, it was still done with a bit of gentleness. But I had noticed he had been getting progressively less gentle since our trip to Aruba in October. Not that I minded at all; in fact, I welcomed it. I liked the feel of choking on his dick; it was turning me all the way on. Didn't matter that I just came, as I was hard all over again.

Suddenly he pulled me off him. I coughed up phlegmy spit all over his thighs. I looked up at him, and he smiled at me. Then he pushed me onto my back again. All too soon, I was lubed up and he was inside of me. He held me by the inside of my thigh in the crook of his elbow and penetrated me deeply. He put his hand around my throat tightly but didn't squeeze, just tight enough to know that he could if he wanted to. Again, I was completely at his mercy, and I loved it. I started begging him, whimpering, scratching him to mimic me fighting him. He understood his role and slammed into me harder. I could tell he lost himself inside of me, in our reluctance play. His grunting was louder, his movements more erratic. Then he leaned over and sucked the inside of my neck right under my chin, then bit me. I was a mess after that, my orgasmic wave completely overwhelmed me. I moaned loudly as I came, my body shaking. He took his hand off my neck and slammed it onto my mouth, making a red mark on my pale skin. Then he began to cum with every pump, moaning, writhing, his own body shaking above me.

When he was done, he let his full weight fall on me again, letting my leg go. I stretched below him, and he put his face in my neck, breathing hard. He licked and sucked my bruised skin gently, and I caressed his back.

I wanted to know what he was thinking. "Jamel? Can I ask you a question?"

"No," he said from inside my neck. "You may not."

I didn't know what to make of that, and his strict tone made me giggle. But I obeyed and just continued to hold onto my husband, both of us wide awake and just enjoying the afterglow of our love.

Jamel and I woke up early Thursday morning, but neither of us wanted to get out of bed just yet. So, we held onto each other and talked about nothing in the dark room. Our schedules didn't allow much opportunity for us to lay around lazily in bed like that, so we took full advantage. I still loved the feel of his skin against mine and the way he gently ran the pad of his fingers up and down my arm or leg. He did it absent-mindedly when we were close, especially when we were naked. I still couldn't get enough of his touch, ten years later.

The first rays of light appeared, and I thought about the first time we were in Miami. I remembered watching the sun hit his dark brown skin as he slept and thinking to myself how much I loved him, just six months into our relationship. I remembered that I told him then when he was fast asleep. It made me kiss his arm and tell him again, while he was wide awake. He smiled at me, rubbed his nose against mine, and kissed my face. He didn't need to say it back, and I didn't need to hear it. He already told me in the gentle way he caressed my skin.

Eventually, I got out of bed and went downstairs to make coffee for the rest of the house, with the intention of bringing a cup back upstairs to him and continuing our snuggle time. But as I was in the kitchen, I heard soft music playing in the backyard. I looked out and there was the Major, doing small movements of tai chi in the grass. He was wearing what looked like silk pajamas and was barefoot. He was graceful for a man at 6'1", his arms and legs moving with fluidity. His eyes were closed, and he was deep into his meditation.

I watched him for a while until the beeping of the coffee machine took me out of my trance. I went over and made Jamel a cup and took it back upstairs to him.

"Thank you, baby," he said, as he took it from me.

"You're welcome, baby," I answered back and kissed him on the lips. "I'll be back."

"Where are you going?" He sort of pouted, also wanting more cuddle time.

I kissed his lips again. "To go spend time with my dad."

He gave me a soft smile. "Okay."

I went downstairs and opened the back door, walking out to the grassy area. The Major still didn't notice me as I stood about two feet behind him and tried to mimic his movements. When my bare feet moved across the grass, making a small sound, he opened his eyes abruptly and turned around. I froze in my stance. He looked at me with an unreadable expression, as expected. Then he faced ahead of him and began moving again. I began to move with him.

I noticed his movements were a tad slower, that he was showing me the steps, teaching me. He ended up doing the same ten moves over and over again until I got the hang of it, and together we began to move in sync. I too closed my eyes and breathed through every motion. I cleared my mind and thought of nothing of importance and followed my father-in-law into mindfulness. The music got lower and ended. I ended up in a fighting stance and opened my eyes. The Major was in the same stance, but he was looking at me. He turned his body to me, put his feet together, clasped his hands, and bowed. I did the same, standing straight up and bowed to him. He began to walk into the house, and I followed him. He had a cup of water on the counter and drank half of it, then handed it to me to drink as well. I did, drinking the rest. He took the cup from me, placed it in the sink, and walked back outside; I again followed him. He went to the couch on the deck and sat down. I sat down next to him.

We didn't speak for the next few minutes, just listened to the birds in the palm trees above us. He spoke first. "How is Angie? And Mary Kate?"

The Major had a good relationship with my sisters too, and it was nice that he asked about them. "They're great," I answered. "Angie is due in a few weeks, and Mary Kate and Dennis are considering adoption."

"Good for them. Give them my regards."

"I will." I let a moment pass, then said, "I think Jamel wants to have children with me."

"And you don't want to have children." He said it as a statement, not a question.

"No. I don't."

He nodded. "One thing I know about my son is that he likes to plan things. He's always had his whole life mapped out. He knew he was going to follow me into the Army, because he wanted to be just like his father. He knew he was going to learn a trade so that no matter what he would have a steady career. He knew he was going to buy a house because homeownership is wealth. He was never sure about marriage, but he knew he was going to have children someday. He was going to raise and mentor children, namely Black boys. It was never part of my plan to be married. And I certainly did not want to have children. Because I knew, after the upbringing that I had, I did not have the capacity to nurture a child because I was never nurtured. Sure, my parents fed and clothed me, but that was all they did. So, I told myself from a very young age that being a father was not in the cards for me. I suspect you did too."

I didn't respond, just let out a sigh through my nose. He continued. "But also like me, Jamel didn't expect to fall in love with someone who was going to derail all his plans. Denita was part of a singing group when we met, a young thing passing through town with her sisters. I'll never forget it: she sang, 'Killing Me Softly,' the Robert Flack version, not that hippy version y'all have out." I chuckled at that. "But she sang it to me. She was barely nineteen at the time, but I bought her a drink and took her to my home, wanting to have my way with her. Instead, she had her way with me, got into my mind and my heart without so much as a kiss on the cheek. By the time the sun rose, I knew I was going to marry that woman and give her as many children as she wanted. After all the things she told me she had been through in her life, I knew my purpose in life was to love her, protect her, and make her happy. Her happiness made me happy. And it still does."

I sighed again. "So, what you're saying is I need to change my plans to make Jamel happy, because he's worth it." And he was right. Jamel was worth it, and I should be more open to giving him the life that he's always wanted just to make him happy. Even if that meant raising children with him.

But The Major surprised me completely. He turned to me and said, "No, Connor. I said Jamel is like me. He's a planner, but he derailed all of his plans the moment you stepped into his life. After everything that you've been through, Jamel knows and believes his purpose in life is to love you, protect you, and make you happy. Because your happiness makes him happy. And it still does."

My mouth opened slightly in confusion. "So, what are you saying? That not having kids makes me happy and he is happy because I'm happy? Or are you saying that I should want to have kids because I know that will make him happy, which will make me happy too?"

The old man just stared at me with amusement in his eyes. "Help me out heeeere," I kinda whined.

He laughed a big laugh, sounding just like my husband. "He doesn't need children to be happy. And you don't need to have children to make him happy, especially if it doesn't make you happy. You and Jamel will be fine, either way, son."

"Well, the last time we talked about it, it didn't seem fine," I mumbled. "I kinda snapped out on him and he just walked away from me, but I knew I hurt him. I had to go back and apologize for being an asshole. I do that a lot."

"Well then don't be an asshole," he said plainly. "Control your emotions. Not everything needs to be an explosive outburst. Most things in life actually don't. Sometimes you don't have to respond. Sometimes you give it to them straight, and then you let it go."

I smiled. "That's what Mel does to me, you know. Just gives it to me straight, then lets it go."

"I know. I taught him well," he said, with a small smile and wink, making me laugh.

We didn't hear his steps until he was right next to us. "Hey, Pop?" Ty said. We both turned to look at him, but he didn't look at me. "Can we talk?"

I started to rise saying, "Sure—"

But The Major cut me off and said, "Not right now, Tyrell. I'm talking to my other son here."

My lips parted, and I resisted the urge to look at either of them, but I quietly sat back down. I watched

Ty walk away from my peripheral vision. As soon as he was out of earshot, I groaned.

"Ugh. You shouldn't have done that, Pop. You know Ty already hates me because of my past relationship with Afia, and this is just going to make it worse, me taking his *daddy* away," I stated, saying that last part sarcastically.

He said, without looking at me, "Tyrell needs to grow up and stop looking for outside threats, focusing on himself and his marriage instead. But that's my job to get that through to him. You just keep being you. And stay out of his way when it comes to Afia."

I nodded. "Sir, yes sir."

CHAPTER 2

BROTHERLY ADVICE

Connor

I joined Afia, Kendra, Vanessa, and Mama Denita in the kitchen preparing food on Thanksgiving Day. I was in charge of the potato salad, which was something very simple that I couldn't fuck up even if I tried. My mother called my phone halfway through the morning. "Hi Connor. Happy Thanksgiving!"

"Happy Thanksgiving, Mom. How's it—"

"Oooh, is that Katie!?" Mama Denita said loudly. "Tell her I'm working on her green bean casserole recipe right now!"

"Oooh, is that Denita?" my mother said happily. "Tell her I made her dressing, but I left out all the cayenne pepper; you know your father and brother aren't good with too much spiciness."

I rolled my eyes, put the phone on speaker, and placed it on the counter, leaving my two mothers to chat away with each other. I listened to them talk about food first, then daytime talk shows like *The View* and *The Talk*. I also had an ear out for the three ladies talking about Rihanna's Fenty line, which complimented Afia's almond brown skin tone to Kendra's caramel one to Vanessa's French vanilla tone. I thought about how content I was, pounding away at the red russet potatoes when Jamel approached me from behind and kissed the side of my neck.

"I'm busy here, go away," I told him playfully.

"Busy making mashed potatoes?" he asked.

"No, this is potato salad," I said with all too much confidence. He reached out and stopped me from pounding it some more. "What?"

"Potato salad is chunky. You're making mashed potatoes."

And of course, everyone in the kitchen heard him, stopped talking, and turned to me. I heard my mother from the phone, "Connor? What did you do?"

Afia walked over and looked into the bowl, then up at me. "He just destroyed the potatoes, Mrs. McIntyre."

"Oh baby, no," Mama Denita said, leaving her casserole and coming over to inspect my destruction.

I looked down into the bowl. "It's not that bad … right?"

Afia, Kendra, and Vanessa started laughing. Jamel came to my rescue. "It's fine, baby. Just boil about five more potatoes and add them in there. Cut them up chunky, don't mash them at all. That should work. Right, Mama?"

She reached over and gave Jamel a hug, her small frame getting no higher than his chest. "I love you, Mel. Thank you."

"You're welcome, Mama," he said, as he hugged her back.

I sighed, got up, and added a few more potatoes to a pot of water and put it on the stove. Then I looked around and realized there was nothing to do until they were boiled. Jamel noticed. "Let's go take a walk."

He held out his hand for me, and I took it. We went out the front entrance and began to walk down the path. "Where you going?" Ty's voice called out. We looked up to see him and his father on the balcony.

"Just going for a quick walk, we'll be back," Jamel answered him.

We didn't talk, just slowly walked through the neighborhood silently, holding hands. There was a time when I would have never done this. I would have been so self-conscious of how others saw me, saw us. So many things have changed to make me stop looking for the approval of others: being with Jamel and seeing how he doesn't notice or care that people know he's gay; coming out officially to my friends and eventually my family; standing up to my father that night at our house when I shot him; even standing up to him during the court hearing, telling my truth and refusing to keep silent on the abuse that I experienced growing up. Every year that passed had me getting further and further away from that scared and insecure boy who was confused about his sexuality. Now I was proud of myself, proud of who I had become.

It made me think of my old therapist, CJ, who on our last visit gave me a little rainbow sticker heart and told me to stick it where I wanted to, as long as I didn't hide it. I came home and put it on Jamel's shirt and told him that he was my rainbow heart, and I would never hide my love from him ever again.

"I'm thinking about writing a book about my life," I said, breaking the silence.

"You should," he replied. "I told you to do that a long time ago."

"I know but ... then I think to myself that it's not going to be a good book. It's going to be awful and have a lot of bad shit in it. No one is going to want to read about abuse and neglect that didn't just happen to me but to other people around me."

"It doesn't matter if it has bad shit in it," he said. "Because it's your truth. The bad shit happened. And you're not the only one who went through bad shit. So maybe you can help other people by calling out the bad shit they too have kept silent about."

He's right, I thought. "That's what I'll name it then. *My Truth, No Longer Keeping Silent.*"

"More like, *The Truth About My Silence.* Because the reason you've been silent is to keep the truth from coming out about everyone else, not just about yourself. You told your truth on the stand back in 2013. But are you prepared to tell everyone else's truth for them? That's what you have to figure out, how to do that."

I was thoughtful. "I don't think I am. Like, I can't tell Vinnie's story, his truth."

"You can, though. You can tell it from your perspective."

I was taking in his words. "Bethany would hate me if I ever did that."

Jamel shrugged. "I don't think she would. Maybe other members of his family, but not Bethany."

"Leo would hate me though. Calling out his father, pulling him out of the closet that no one knew he was in? That's not fair to them. Nah. I couldn't do it," I decided. And just as quickly as that idea came, it flushed away.

Jamel said, "Connor, you ever thought that you keeping silent and not talking about the things you've been through was what was holding you back from being a proud, openly gay man?"

"I am a proud, openly gay man," I said with some indignation. "I was just thinking to myself how far along I've come with that."

He nodded. "Yes, you have." He lifted our hands up to his mouth to kiss mine, making me blush but I let him. Jamel continued. "But I'm just saying, maybe if you would have told someone about the abuse you experienced while it was happening, you would have felt freer to come out a long time ago."

"But if I had talked about it back then, I would have to talk about Matty's abuse and MK's abuse, and my mother's too. How could I have done that?"

"Which proves my point: you've been keeping silent to protect those around you, not just yourself. Maybe it's time to free your voice."

I was quiet after that, and he let me think about it some more. *Maybe one day, but I'm not ready yet. And neither was anyone else for what I had to say.*

♥

Thankfully, I didn't botch the potato salad and the table looked great. Ten adults and six children gathered around the very long, live oak table and held hands. The Major said grace, and the side dishes began to be passed around. He let Mel cut one turkey and Ty cut the other one, and as usual, Ty and Donny argued over who was getting the bigger turkey leg, but since Ty had the knife, he won. I briefly thought of my family having Thanksgiving at Owen's house, the house I had not stepped foot into in seven years. They would have been halfway through dinner by the time we got started in Miami. Angie wasn't there; she had planned to go to Nyack to spend it with Chad's family instead of her own. She, like me, didn't really have anything to do with the McIntyres unless she absolutely had to, and mostly for the sake of our mother.

I was getting lost in my thoughts when I heard The Major call to me, "Connor? You okay, son?"

Jamel looked over at me with concern. Ty did too, not with concern but more with a grimace. I smiled at my father-in-law. "I'm doing great, Pop. Thanks."

I reached over for my mediocre potato salad and gave myself a heaping, waiting for Jamel to put turkey on my plate.

"The grands got the kids so we're free," Donny said hours later, as we sat around the pool. "Vanessa and I are headed to the strip tonight. Who's coming with?"

"Jamel and I are down," I spoke for him, to which he shrugged in agreement.

"We're going for romance tonight," said Lavell and reached over to hold Kendra's hand. "Y'all go have fun."

"Ty and I will go," Afia said. "We need to not be parents for a few hours."

And that was how our night began. Since it was six of us, we piled up in our rental, parked at 16th and Collins, then walked down to Atlantic. It was a nice crowd in the streets and in every restaurant and lounge there. We started out together but slowly broke into smaller groups: Jamel and Ty, Donny and Vanessa, and Afia and I. Afia and I stopped in every restaurant and bar and took a shot. By the fourth one, we both had a nice buzz going and found ourselves laughing loudly, dancing in the street, and having a good time.

We stopped near the clock tower. "Take sexy pictures of me. I want to feel sexy," Afia said, as she faced the wall, lifted up her leg, and turned to me over her shoulder.

I laughed and took a picture, saying, "You've always been sexy, Lovie."

"Naaaah! You know that's not true back then or now. Moms aren't sexy." She turned around and did another pose where she was crouched, and her legs were open.

I took another pic. "There is literally a whole acronym for you: MILF. You're a MILF."

She stood up and frowned. Then she grabbed both her boobs, squeezed them upward, and opened her mouth seductively. I laughed out loud and took a few more pics. I didn't see him as he rushed past me, only when he was right on her.

Ty said, "That's enough, Fi. You had too much to drink, and we're going back."

"She's fine," I told him. "Afia doesn't get drunk; she knows her limits." Tyrell ignored me and yanked my friend by her arm, pulling her closer to him. "Yo, what the fuck!?" I yelled at him. I didn't like that one bit and instinctively began to walk toward him in anger.

"What!" he yelled back and walked even quicker toward me. He got in my face and said, "You gonna tell me about my wife again?"

"What the *fuck* is your problem, Ty?" I said nastily, my chest burning in anger.

Afia stood to the side of us and said, "Tyrell, what is going on?"

He turned to look at her. "I don't like who you are tonight. We talked about this." I caught that "this" meant me. They talked about our "fake-ass friend-ship" again.

She said back, "And I don't like who you've been since we were on the plane. You've been nothing but aggressive to Connor. So I'm going to ask again, what is going on?"

He slowly turned back to me and said, "I don't need your advice about my wife, Connor. I don't need you to tell me when she needs breaks or if she has or hasn't had too much to drink. If Afia has an issue with anything I'm saying or doing, she can talk to me. You're not her bodyguard. You're not her husband. You're just a friend. Know your role. Stay in your place."

I tried to see in my head what he was seeing regarding me telling him what to do, and I honestly wasn't trying to. If it was anyone else, I would have the same reaction regarding Afia. She was my friend, but she is and will always be so much more to me than that, so I did feel a sense of protection over her, even from her husband. But I also realized that Afia and I don't hang out around Ty for this very reason. He gets tense when we're around each other, and he saw things that weren't there. I'd tried to be patient with this whole thing, but I was honestly getting sick of his attitude.

"Actually, I'm her brother now," I said with a smile. "So, I still get to protect her."

He practically spit in my face, "And I'm her husband. You don't get to speak for her, I do. And the next time you give me some of your *brotherly* advice about *my* wife, we're gonna have a problem."

I saw Mel, Donny, and Vanessa begin to walk over to us, and I knew that was my cue, once again, to back down. I nodded and said, "Cool." I stepped around him and walked toward my husband.

I heard Afia say, "What is wrong with you!? Connor is right. I'm not drunk. And I'm not going anywhere with you. You can go back home if you'd like."

She also stepped around him and walked up to the rest of the group. He followed her, saying, "I'm not leaving you here, Fi."

"Then stay, but if you're going to stay, then stop being a DICK!" she yelled at him. "I just want one night to not be a mom. Can I have one fucking night off!?"

"I'll give you one night!" someone yelled in the crowd behind us and others laughed. I couldn't help but smile.

"Hey, how about this?" Jamel said, stepping in, feeling the tension in the air, and taking charge. "How about Afia and Vanessa, you ladies get lost and go have some fun? The four of us will find something else to get into. We'll meet at the truck in two hours. Deal?"

"That sounds great," Vanessa said happily, also trying to defuse the tension. "Let's go not be moms for a little while." She smiled at Afia, who smiled back and walked her away from the rest of us.

When they were out of earshot, Donny put his hand on Ty's shoulder and said, "You gotta chill, bro. Take a lesson from Pop. He never held reigns on Mama, and their relationship is solid. I don't put reigns on anyone. Let her be an individual, and she'll come back to you sweeter than ever before."

He shook his head. "I'm not trying to put reigns on her. Afia can do what she wants. I just don't like how she is when she's around certain people. Drinking more and acting like she ain't got no sense."

"Certain people like me?" I asked.

He looked at me and came closer. "Yeah. I don't like how she is when she's around you."

I nodded again. "Cool. Well, she's not around me anymore so you don't have to worry about that, right?" I took Jamel's hand and turned around before he could answer.

We walked in silence for a moment, then Jamel said quietly, "Thank you."

I didn't respond.

♥

Friday night, we found ourselves in the living room downstairs, the Jones brothers and me. Jamel said, "I'm going to go find Pop," and left us. He was the last one to have one-on-one time with The Major. Donny lit a joint as expected and passed it around, but only Lavell participated a little. Ty opted out, wanting to nurse his drink instead. I did the same, not wanting to be high at the moment.

"So, what's up with you and Vanessa?" Ty asked. "Because I swore I heard some noises coming from your room."

"Nah, that was Connor and Jamel's room," Lavell teased.

"That's a fucking lie," I said with a smile. "We've been quiet."

"A little too quiet. Can't tell who's fucking who anymore," Donny said, making me laugh out loud.

"Do you really want to know?" Ty asked, with a look of disgust on his face.

Donny thought about it. "Probably not."

"Probably!?" Lavell and I exclaimed at the same time, and we all laughed again.

We were quiet for a moment, then Donny took a drag and said, as he breathed out, "We're poly now. Vanessa and I are poly."

Ty was confused. "Poly? Polygamy? You convince her to let you get another wife?"

"No, polyamorous. Not polygamy," Donny explained. "I'm not married to anyone, but I do have two relationships."

"What the fuck is the difference?" asked Ty, all confused.

Lavell spoke up, "Polyamory. From the Latin: Poly meaning many, and the Greek: Amorous meaning loves. It's the opposite of monogamy; you have multiple simultaneous relationships and partners. Polygamy is many marriages. Polyamory is many lovers." Everyone just turned to look at him, always stunned when he spouted out information. He shrugged. "I read a lot."

That made us all laugh, but I was curious. "So, what does that mean, Donny? That you're seeing each other but she allows you to see other people?"

"It's not an allowance. She has other relationships too. Right now, we're in a quad. We don't live together, but she's my primary. She has a boyfriend, Rahiem; he and I are friends, metamours. Vanessa and I share a girlfriend, Tania. Tania and I are trying to get pregnant."

"Whoa, whoa, whoa, back this up for me," I started, as confused as everyone else.

"Back this up for all of us!" said Ty. "You and Vanessa are together again?"

"Yes." He puffed out smoke.

I started, "But Vanessa has a side piece—"

"No," he cut me off. "Rahiem is not a side piece. He's her partner. And I'm her partner."

Lavell asked, "But you have another partner, Tania?"

"Yup."

"And you and Vanessa *share* her?" Ty asked. "What does that mean?"

"Exactly what it sounds like," he said in all seriousness. "She spends time individually with me and individually with her. Sometimes all three of us."

"So, basically, y'all having threesomes," I deduced.

He shook his head and sat all the way up. "No, you're missing it. I love them both. And they love each other. We're in a triad. It's not about sex. We have a real, solid relationship of love, admiration, and appreciation. Vanessa and I rarely have sex but we're always together. And Tania and I built something special over the last two years. She came into the situation with Vanessa and I and just embraced her and embraced my son. She's amazing. Vanessa fell in love with her too, and they began building a relationship, outside of me. We rarely have threesomes, because I want my individual time with Tania, and so does Vanessa."

I was fascinated. I've heard about poly relationships, but it all seemed so complicated, and just another reason for a man to have two girlfriends. To hear that Vanessa basically has two boyfriends and everyone was okay with it was fascinating. "So where does Rahiem fit into all this?" I asked.

"Rahiem is new to being poly. He came into Vanessa's life about six months ago and is still trying to understand it all. But he's learning and wants to be a part of it because he loves Vanessa too. We all do. She's the center of our polycule."

"So do Tania and Rahiem have sex?" Lavell asked.

"No," he said. "But with Rahiem, we are a quad. Tania is my and Vanessa's partner. Rahiem is Vanessa's partner. He doesn't desire a relationship with Tania and Tania's only male partner is me, her choice for now."

"But what if that changes and she wants to start fucking other men too?" Ty asked. "How would you feel about that?"

Donny shrugged. "She could now if she wants to. I told you, I don't hold reigns on anyone. She is a free poly woman."

"This is stupid," Ty said dismissively. "What about love, marriage, family, commitment?"

"We have all of that, bro," Donny said back. "We all love each other and we're a family. But marriage is a social construct, a legal contract. We don't need to be legally bound to each other to have commitment, and we do have commitment. We are committed to each other."

"How are y'all committed when they both out there fucking other men?" Ty said, astounded. "I couldn't imagine letting my wife fuck other men."

"That's because you're an alpha male with toxic masculinity," Donny said casually and took another puff.

Lavell and I both chuckled at that. But Ty turned to me and said, "Just the thought of her fucking someone else makes me want to choke the shit out of him."

I scoffed and looked away. *I'm not taking the bait.*

"That's your issue," said Donny. "Your insecurity. What me and Vanessa have, no one could take away. When she's with Rahiem, I'm not worried about him taking her away or her falling deeper in love with him than with me. I'm not worried about whether he makes love to her better than me. The love she has for me is between us. Her relationship with him doesn't change that for us. And she isn't threatened by Tania and our love. She wants us to procreate. She doesn't plan on having other children, but it makes her happy to know that it would make Tania and me happy to have a child together. I'm not selfish about my partner's happiness. Any of them."

We were all quiet, all lost in our own thoughts. Threesomes were okay; Jamel and I had a spectacular one while in Aruba just a month ago and I wouldn't shy away from doing it again. But I couldn't do what Donny was doing. I couldn't open up our marriage and allow Jamel to fall in love with someone else. That's what Nick did, opened their relationship up so he could fuck around, and all it did was show Jamel what else was out there, pulling him further away. There was no way I could chance that. Donny was right; it is about insecurity. As far as I had come, I was way too insecure within myself. And I was okay with that level of insecurity.

I spoke first. "Honestly, I love that for you, and her and everyone involved. But I couldn't do it. I've had multiple partners before and didn't care if they had partners. But now that I'm monogamous and married, this is better for me. I love that you have the capacity to love more than one person and be all accepting, but I'm with Ty. You can call it insecurity, but Jamel provides that security for me, and that's what I need. Just the thought of Jamel loving someone else other than me, I wouldn't be able to handle it. The fucking garbage man on our block flirts with Jamel, and I'm resisting the urge to grab my gun every Wednesday morning."

My brothers chuckled and I did too, but said, "I'm serious, man. But I'm happy for you. Both of you. All … of you?" I said it purposely in a confused tone, and they laughed. "Whatever, if you love it, I love it for you." I shrugged and Donny chuckled again.

Lavell asked, "Does Pop know?"

"Yeah. I told him when Tania, Vanessa, and I officially entered into a triad. I wanted to bring her this weekend, but she said it was fine; she didn't want to intrude just yet. That's why we're headed back early; we're going to spend some time with her family. She'll be here next year though, for sure."

"And he was accepting of all this free love you got going on?" Ty asked.

"Well, he wasn't happy about it at first. But we talked about it some more last night, and I think he understands. He told me to make sure I don't intentionally hurt anyone, and to always be upfront and honest about my lifestyle with everyone I meet. Get tested regularly and treat the ladies with respect. It was good advice. He always gives good advice."

"Yeah," I agreed. "He really does."

We heard footsteps coming down and thought it was Mel, but it was Kendra. She leaned over the rail and said, "Lavell, come to bed."

Lavell stood up and stretched. "That's my cue. You gentlemen have a good night."

"Yeah, not as good as you're about to have," Donny said, with amusement in his voice.

"Bout to make some more babies, huh?" I said with a smile.

Lavell ignored the teasing, gave us all a dap, and followed his wife upstairs. It was quiet until Donny finished his joint and said, "I'm going to bed too. We have an early flight."

"Cool, I'll head up too," Ty said, standing up.

But I said, "Ty? Can we talk for a moment?"

Ty looked like he wanted to do anything but talk to me. But Donny gave him a little shove on his shoulder and said, "Good night, Connor."

"Good night, Donny," I responded. Ty sat back down across from me. "Hey, listen. I'm sorry if you feel like I'm overstepping my boundaries when it comes to Afia."

"You *are* overstepping," he cut me off. "I don't think you are; you are. And I don't appreciate it."

"Okay, and I'm sorry," I said quickly. "I do get protective over her, I'll admit that. She's been my best friend for the last twenty years of my life, so it's hard to let go. But I feel like I've been doing a good job of it." I kinda smiled at him, but he didn't smile back. I sighed. "What do I need to do to make you feel comfortable about our friendship? Because Ima be honest; it's never going to change. She's always going to be my person, and I am hers. And like Donny just said, that doesn't take anything away from what you have with her. Which, I'm reminding you again, is deeper and stronger than anything we've ever had."

"So, when you and Afia were fucking, it was just sex?" he asked.

I opened my mouth slightly. *So many things wrong with that statement.* "Afia and I weren't *fucking*. I took her virginity when we were teenagers because she asked me to. Then years after that, we had one night and never did it again. And that was over a decade ago. We weren't friends with benefits. We were just friends. Only friends." And it wasn't just sex, but there was no way I was going to tell him that.

Ty scoffed. "I don't know who you think you're fooling, Connor. But you were in love with her back then, and you're still in love with her now."

I shook my head. "I'm in love with your brother."

Ty scoffed again. "You can be in love with two people at the same time. Ain't that what Donny is doing right now?"

I shook my head again. "I'm not in love with Afia. I do love her, but not in the way you think. Not in the way you love her. And more importantly, she's in love with you, not me."

"Oh, I know she's in love with me," he said cockily. "There is nothing you can do for her that I can't do ten times better, and then some. I'm what she wants and what she needs, not you."

"Then why do we keep having a problem?" I gritted through my teeth.

"Because I don't trust you!" he blurted out. "Not just with my wife. I don't trust you with my brother either. I've known guys like you my whole life. It's in your nature to want to fuck someone else, and getting married to him ain't gonna change your nature."

I practically laughed at him. "We've been together for ten years, Tyrell. I'm not going to cheat on him and I'm never leaving him. So, you're wrong."

"It's just a matter of time," he said, so sure of himself. "And once that happens, I'll be happy to see you gone from my family."

I shook my head. "Not gonna happen. You're stuck with me. I'm your brother too."

He stood up. "You're not my brother, Connor. You may have gotten everyone else fooled, my pop, my mama, my brothers, my wife, even my children, but I see right through you. You're selfish. You go for what you want, and you don't care about anyone else's feelings. That sleeping dragon in you is going to wake up one day and you're going to slip up. And the day you hurt Jamel, I'm coming for you."

He started to walk away when I said, "And I see right through you, Ty. You're an insecure little boy with daddy issues. That's not attractive to her. And if you keep that up, you're going to lose her. Just a little *brotherly* advice." He turned around and walked up to me. I stood up.

"Fuck you, Connor," he said nastily. "I should knock you the fuck out right now."

I still had my glass of bourbon in my hand. I visualized smashing it over his head. Or I could continue to provoke him into hitting me so I would have a reason to kick the shit out of him. But then I remembered that everything didn't need to be an emotional outburst. I had already said all I needed to say, and it was time to let it go. My father taught me that.

So instead, I raised my glass to my lips and took a small sip, keeping my eye on him. "Good night, Tyrell," I said calmly.

We stared at each other. He turned first to walk away. As he walked up the stairs, I said, "One day you'll realize I'm not the monster you think I am. I just hope it's not too late. For Afia and Jamel's sake."

He didn't respond, just kept walking. I sat back down and drank some more, thinking about how much I wanted to punch my brother-in-law in the face, but knowing I never would. I must have fallen asleep because the next thing I knew, Jamel was tapping me awake and leading me to bed.

CHAPTER 3

CAN I BE PISSED AT YOU?

Jamel

The door was stubborn, as sometimes oak is. But I knew I just needed to take my time with it. I gently used the sandpaper strip to shave down the sides. One third of an inch was to be removed so that it would fit better. Darius, my worker, wanted to cut it, but I took the job from him. I thought about nothing, feeling at home working with my hands and listening to the rain hitting the window. I had been on this one piece of wood for hours, and that was okay. The door to the sunroom was going to be perfect.

Ty came knocking on the door. "Storm is coming in. I'm sending the guys home."

"Okay," I replied without looking up and continued sanding. I felt him watching me, but then he left.

I was almost done so I wasn't going to stop. Ty came back about fifteen minutes later. "Mel, it's icy rain coming down. Let's go."

Again, I didn't look up. "Okay."

He walked over and stood in front of me. "It looks good. Pop would be proud. Now can we go before the street turns into an ice-skating rink?"

I leaned up and put the sander down. "He looked good, didn't he?"

Tyrell sat on a crate. "He did. He looked happy too, like the stress was completely off him. Not a worry in the world. It was the right decision for them to move down there."

"Yeah. I still miss him though. Mama too."

Ty took a moment, then said, "I gotta say, these last couple of years without him ... I miss him but ... I feel like I can breathe for the first time in my life."

I nodded in understanding. My brother and my father's relationship had not always been the best. Ty tested every bit of him growing up, always getting into trouble. And my father was hard on him, always making sure he knew that he never measured up, even into adulthood.

I asked, "So what did you talk about on the balcony?"

"He was just asking how everything was going with the house, kids. We talked about Afia a lot, how relationships change after having kids, but to keep at it. Asked a little about work. I told him it was all good here."

"Did he tell you he was proud of you again?"

Ty scoffed. "Of course not. We only get one of those a lifetime." I chuckled but he looked at me. "Did he tell you he's proud of you? Because I always feel like he says it to the rest of you and not me."

I looked back at him sarcastically. "You know he doesn't do that. I just know that he is. He's proud of both of us."

"True," Ty agreed. "I swear I'm going to be different with my kids though. I'll tell them every day that I love them. Give them affirmations, tell them they are doing a good job. None of us really got that growing up. That's just how Pop is; it's like he doesn't have it in him."

"Well, he does give Connor a little more affirmation than he does us though. But that's probably because he feels like Connor needs it more from a father figure." As soon as I said the words, I knew I walked into it.

Ty's mouth curled up in almost a snarl. "More than his own sons? Just giving that white boy special treatment, huh?"

I kept my cool and said, "That white boy is my husband."

Ty blinked at me twice. "Yeah. Don't I know it." He stood up and said, as he walked out, "Don't stay much longer. Lock up behind you."

"Sure thing, Boss."

Ty would never admit it, but I believe one of the reasons he didn't like Connor was because of how close he and our father were. It may have started with his jealousy and insecurity over Connor's history with Afia, but it was deeper than that for him. Connor has a great relationship with every single member of my family and fit in so easily right from the beginning. And they've just gotten closer over the years, especially

Connor and my pop, which was a real sore spot for Ty. My brother is my best friend, so it had been rough trying to navigate their cold war. I asked Connor to be the bigger person when it came to Ty, and I am thankful that he was. But every once in a while, Ty would make his true feelings known, like he did on Thanksgiving. Mostly I ignored it, except the moments when Ty became dangerously close to being insulting or disrespectful as he did then.

I looked back at my work and then up at the darkening sky. It was only about 1:30 p.m., but the day was over for me. I locked up the house we were renovating and hopped in my truck to head home. Usually, I come in through the garage and make my way upstairs from inside, but I wanted to head back out and do some grocery shopping so I could make dinner before Connor got home. So, instead, I parked on the street and came in through the front door. As soon as I did, I heard the loud music and knew at least one of the Four Musketeers was in the basement.

I went downstairs and opened the door to the media room. I saw them before they saw me: Connor's nephew Freddie was on top of my friend's daughter Kim, his shirt off and pubescent body exposed, while her shirt was off and her pink bra barely on, making out.

These kids can't be fucking serious. "YO!" I yelled loudly, and they both jumped up.

"Oh shit! Uncle Mel! Shit!" Freddie exclaimed as he looked around, threw Kim's sweater at her, and struggled to put his long-sleeved shirt on.

I went over to the stereo system and turned off the music, which I now identified as smooth R&B. *Ain't that fucking nice.* I walked out, saying over my shoulder, "Get dressed and come upstairs, now."

Honestly, I wasn't sure how to handle it. I've known Kim all her life, being that her mothers were close friends of mine. Chantel and Shawn trust me with their thirteen-year-old daughter and if something were to happen to her on my watch, they would both kill me. The last thing these two women needed was for their daughter to end up pregnant.

And then my nephew was such a troubled kid whose parents hated me and tolerated Connor. But even if both of them had completely uncomplicated families, they are thirteen and fourteen years old! *What the fuck are they doing?*

They came upstairs looking embarrassed and sheepish. I decided I wasn't going to address it yet. "Go get your coats and get in my truck. We're going food shopping." Freddie rolled his eyes, but Kim turned around abruptly to go back downstairs.

"Uncle Mel—" Freddie started.

"Don't talk, Freddie. Don't … talk. Just go get your coat," I told him sternly.

He sighed and followed Kim, then they both met me at my truck. We drove to the grocery store in silence, then I delegated tasks, putting Kim on fruits and vegetables and sending Freddie to the pasta aisle, on opposite sides of ShopRite. We drove back home in silence until I said, "One of you is going to help me cook while the other cleans up the media room. Pick."

"Well, Kim can help you cook," Freddie said automatically.

She snapped at him. "Why, because I'm a girl?" She didn't wait for his response as she turned to me and said, "I'll clean up downstairs, Uncle Mel."

"I didn't mean it like that," he said to her softly.

"Shut up, Fredrick," she retorted. I resisted the urge to smile at her using his proper name.

While Freddie stirred the pasta in the pot and I sauteed the chicken, we were quiet until he asked me, "Please don't tell Uncle Connor. He's gonna be pissed at me."

I looked at him like he lost his mind and snapped at him. "Are you insane? I could never keep something like this from him. And what the fuck were you thinking!? You told me you weren't having sex! Are you two having sex?"

"No!" he denied. "But … would it be so bad if I was? Or is it because it's Kim? Because she's Black? Or maybe I'm not good enough for her because of … my dad?"

I lost some of my anger at the situation. Connor's brother Matthew was an asshole to everyone, including his own son. It pissed me off, but I tried really hard to stay out of Connor's family drama and let him handle his brother's antics when it came to Freddie. *Because if I get involved, I'm going to end up murdering that sonofabitch.*

I told him, "Freddie, it's because you are too young. And I'm not just saying that because it's the thing adults say. I'm saying it because you barely have hair on your chest, how could you ever think you would be mentally and emotionally ready for sex?"

"I heard Uncle Connor say he lost his virginity at thirteen," he mumbled.

"And your Uncle Connor would probably be the first one to tell you that he was not emotionally ready for that at that age, trust me. But since you need to hear it firsthand, I will let him talk to you about it. For now, I'm going to say this: I don't care about Kim being your girlfriend. It has nothing to do with her being Black. I do care about her being used by you so you can just get your rocks off and leave her behind if something were to happen to her. Because here's the deal: if you aren't ready to be a father at fourteen, then you aren't ready to have sex. Period."

I looked him in the eyes and waited for his response. "I don't want to talk about this anymore," he mumbled again as he looked down.

"Right. Reason number three why you shouldn't be having sex. You can't even talk about it in a mature way. So, until you can, don't do it." I turned back to my chicken, leaving the conversation alone for now.

When Connor came home, Freddie looked at me with fearful eyes, but I ignored him. I followed my husband upstairs as he changed into comfortable clothing to tell him what happened and about the conversation Freddie and I just had. His eyes bugged out of his head.

"Holy shit!"

"I know."

He sat on the edge of the bed, looking thoughtful. "Okay. Okay, I'll handle it. I'll talk to him."

"And I'll talk to Kim when I give her a ride home." She lived less than nine miles away, which was usually fine but in this weather, I would never let her go by herself.

We went downstairs and Freddie looked like he was ready to throw up, waiting to be chastised. Instead, Connor casually sat down for dinner, so he relaxed. It was pretty silent as the four of us ate, then Connor started talking.

"When I was thirteen, Matty had this girlfriend, Rachel. My friends and I had just discovered *Playboy* magazines. One day, I was masturbating in the bathroom to one, and she walked in and wouldn't leave. Not until I finished."

I didn't react but Freddie and Kim both looked horrified and embarrassed at this conversation. That did not stop Connor from talking. "The next day, she came to find me in the house without Matty around and told me I had a big cock for my age. She was sixteen. Fast forward a couple of weeks; she cornered me and gave me my first blowjob, unrequested. She would continue to do so every time Matty wasn't around until she took it a step further and got on top of me one day; that was my first sexual experience. I know now that what happened to me was molestation, something boys don't talk about."

He paused and let his words sink in. "I turned fourteen a couple months later and started high school, where got my first girlfriend, Abby. It didn't take me long to start pushing her for sex. I took her virginity when I knew she wasn't ready, and frankly neither was I, but because I had already done it, or had it done to me, I didn't think anything of it. We did it two more times, and then I broke up with her to try again with someone else. I spent a lot of years hurting a lot of people, using people for sex, all the way into my twenties, all because of what was done to me as a kid, among other things."

He looked Freddie in the eyes. "You should *never* want to be like me. Ever."

Freddie was still wide-eyed, but he nodded. We continued to eat in silence, then Connor asked, "What about EJ and Imani? Are they having sex?"

Kim and Freddie started laughing. Kim answered, "No, they're still pretending like they don't like each other."

Connor smiled and said, "So it's a *Dawson's Creek* situation?"

"Who's Dawson's Creek?" Freddie asked.

"Is that a new reality show?" Kim asked.

Connor looked at me, stunned. I laughed and said, "You're old, man."

Connor and I typically don't do anything for New Year's Eve, as we spend November and December holidays running back and forth between our families. So, since the beginning of our relationship, we've kept this holiday just for us. We usually spend it in bed together, literally fucking into the new year, but this year we agreed to spend it with my friends Josh and Willy at Bulldogs, a famous nightclub in Atlanta, Georgia. Even Henry and Tosha came out to join us at the LGBTQ spot, dancing all night to hip-hop and house music to ring in the New Year. We hadn't been out since we went to Aruba, and I started thinking about all we did, including with Romy. I know Connor was thinking about it too, especially when the reggae and dancehall music started, because he looked at me with this shit-eating grin on his face and pulled me closer.

We kissed, then he asked in my ear, "No regrets?"

I pulled him back so he could see my face. I shook my head and mouthed, "None." He smiled at me and leaned forward to kiss again. Back at Josh's house, we made love quietly, in contrast to Josh and Willy's ridiculously loud fucking all night, which made us laugh.

I woke up and was surprised to see that Connor was not under me. He wasn't even in the bed; he must have woken up much earlier than I did and quietly snuck out. I laid there for a moment and thought about Nick, my best friend of twenty years who died last August. He would have loved last night. His favorite pastime besides sex was dancing until the sun came up. He would call me in the middle of the night from some club, yelling into the phone, "Wish you were here, Jay Jones!" I smiled to myself through my heartache. I still miss him so much it hurts.

I found a pen and paper and wrote to him:

Damn Nicky·

Can I be pissed at you? Because I think I still am· You're the one person in my life I never had to explain myself to, never had to hide my emotions from· Now who am I going to complain to when Connor pisses me off? Or talk to when he does something that makes me fall more in love with him? I mean, did you see us in Aruba? You would have enjoyed me reliving that experience with you· I would have told you everything, every sordid detail, make you envious of Connor and I· But there is no one I could tell that story to now· So like so many other things, I'll just keep it inside unless Connor wants to talk about it· He hasn't just yet, and I don't know if he ever will· Connor still keeps parts of himself inside, even from me· I just want him to feel comfortable being exactly who he is at all times with me· I have to find a way to bring it out of him, that side he still wants to keep hidden from me· I feel like this might be something he would want to do from time to time, and I would be down with it, but I want him to be more open with me about this. How do I get him to be more open with me? You've helped me so much over the years with how to draw a guy like Connor closer to me. Who's going to help me figure out how to do that now?

I was thinking the other day about the last time I saw you, at my wedding ceremony. You were starting to gray, and I told you that you were getting old. And you said to me, "I feel younger every day with him." That made me smile. It still makes me smile, just thinking about how happy you were with Josh. I'm worried about him, still. I know he still feels the loss, the big Nicky size hole in his life that nothing will ever fill. But we're going to try to, for you. We're going to put him under our wing and make him a part of us, make sure he knows that he has family, he has us. Being around Josh, being someone he is able to lean on, helps me feel close to you. I *want you to know that I will always be there for him, just like you were there for me.*

I miss you. I think about you several times a day. I listen to your old voice messages on my phone, and it makes me cry that I'll never hear your voice again. It hurts so much. I think about you dying in Kandahar of all places, the same place we lost Cliff back in 2003. You and I barely made it out of there alive. You didn't die then and weren't supposed to die now, asshole. You were supposed to grow old, be my person like Meredith and Christina on Grey's Anatomy, our favorite show. I'm so pissed at you. You were so many things to me: a first lover, a best friend, a big brother, a confidant. I lost all those things in one moment, and I'm so fucking pissed off at you. But also, I forgive you for leaving me on this earth without you. I'm mad. And I forgive you—

I couldn't write anymore; the tears were blinding me, so I put the pen down and wiped them away. I sat there at the edge of the bed with my eyes closed, as the tears continued to fall. Connor's voice filtered into my head, telling me to visualize the waves of the ocean, to breathe in and breathe out until my breath mimicked the sound of the waves on the sand. It was a meditation he started the day with sometimes, if he woke up and felt off. I've never been a meditator until Connor came into my life, and now I'm grateful. In those moments, I saw the value in grounding yourself, finding your balance. I didn't know how long I sat there, but by the time I opened my eyes, my heart hurt a little less. Just a minuscule.

I washed my face, put on clothes, and went looking for Connor, finding him and Josh out front on the steps talking. The weather wasn't nearly as cold as it should have been for January 1st. It felt like spring down there.

"Hey," Connor said. He watched me come closer with those blue eyes of his so full of love for me.

"Hey," I said back, as I sat on the step above him. I hadn't brushed my teeth yet, but that didn't stop him from leaning up and kissing my lips. I rolled my fingers through his short crop as he leaned back into me. He was letting it grow in just a little, and I hoped he didn't want to cut it again.

Josh looked at us with envy. "I miss it, being with someone like that. I miss him."

He turned away. Connor asked, "What about you and Willy? I thought you loved him too?"

He rolled his eyes and said, "C'mon." Then he relented and turned back to Connor. "That's not true. I do love him. Just not the way I loved Nicky, you know.

I could never love anyone like that again. I don't think I'll ever stop loving him."

"Then don't," I said. "There is no rule that says you have to stop loving him to move on."

"And it doesn't have to be the same, you know," Connor said. "You can love them both, differently. You can make room in your heart for both, if that's what you want to do. But you also can … you know … walk away from this too."

"From Willy? He'd hunt me down and tie me up in his basement first," Josh said, and we laughed. "Nah, I'm okay where I am for now. Willy makes me feel … normal if that makes sense. Makes the hole in my heart a little smaller. Just a minuscule." That made me smile inside. *Nicky must be listening.*

He was quiet for a moment, then said, "I caught Willy crying about a month ago in the bathroom. He kept apologizing to me, like his own grief didn't matter. I told him he didn't need to be strong for me all the time, pretending like he wasn't hurting. That he could lean on me too. I think that was the turning point for us. I'm not just his promise to Nick anymore, and he's not just something for me to keep busy. So yeah, I love him."

Josh stood up. "I'm going to go hang out with Nicky, tell him about last night. He would have loved it."

Josh walked behind the house toward the field, leaving us alone. We were quiet for a moment, listening to the sounds of grasshoppers, crickets, birds chirping, and little animals scurrying for their morning meals.

Then Connor said, "I could live here, you know. Rural. I thought about asking you last time we were here if you would consider moving to Georgia. Be closer to Josh and Henry. And Will now, too."

I shrugged. "It's an option. But I'm kind of the head of my family now since my parents moved to Florida. Kind of like you are for your sisters too. And since we're leading our families, I'm not so sure we could just pack up and go. It's not just our physical presence but our home too. Freddie and even EJ kind of depend on us. So, I don't know."

"Yeah. That's kinda where I left it too in my thoughts. That we're needed where we are, by everyone. But when we are ready to just pack up and go, I say the first stop should be Aruba."

I laughed. "I would love to retire on an island with you." I could see him smiling from the top of his head.

Of course thoughts of Aruba brought back thoughts of Romy and that threesome we had. I got to see a side of Connor that I had never seen before; as nasty and sadistic as he wanted to be, especially after he got high as a fucking kite. Now I know why he called himself a cum slut, because anywhere there was cum, he was going for it to lick it up. And I always knew Connor liked a little masochism, but his tolerance for pain was higher than I thought. He wanted to be bitten everywhere, demanded it from us, and we gave it to him. But he also wanted to bite back. Romy got most of that, but I let him bite me too here and there. Connor also wanted to be choked until he damn near passed out, which, I had to admit, threw me off. I didn't choke him, also not my thing, but I let Romy do it, despite every nerve in my body wanting to pull his hands from around my husband's throat.

And I was even more nervous when he did the same to Romy, but he knew just enough pressure to apply and when to let go. I told Connor I would let him do what he wanted without judgment from me, so I held to that agreement the whole night.

And I had no regrets since I also got to do what I wanted, with no reservations. My dick forgot that it was thirty-eight years old, and it stayed hard inside of both men all night, stretching out their holes, fisting one while fucking the other, then switching. At one point, Connor sat back smoking a joint, watching me hardcore fuck another man with a grin on his face the whole time. And not just watch, but doing his dirty talk, encouraging me, egging me on, slapping my ass. It was a wild and sex-crazed night. And in the morning, when Romy left our room, we were still Jamel and Connor, more in love with each other than the day before, and more secure and trusting in our relationship, because we decided together and experienced it all together. Since Aruba, I'd been giving him a little more of it, the pain with the pleasure that I now know he likes, almost craves. My way of showing him I was accepting of who he is. And in return, he began kissing me on the front porch of our home before work, instead of inside the house. His way of being more open, and it made my heart happy. Although the lengthier tongue kissing on Wednesdays might have more to do with Jon the sanitation man too.

I found my opening to talk about Aruba. "You miss it?" I asked him.

He hesitated, then asked, "The island? Yeah."

I smiled. "And him?" I leaned over and kissed the side of my husband's face.

Connor hesitated again, then said, "Maybe a little. Maybe not him exactly, but … maybe the thrill of it all."

I nodded. "Same. I don't know if it was Romy or being with another person in general that made me feel so much sexual energy. But I'm so glad we got to do it together."

He let a moment pass, then said, "Maybe it was Romy a little. Because he was hot, so fucking hot," he said dreamily.

I started laughing and nodded, agreeing with my lover and best friend. "That he was. Fucking hot."

"Would you do it again with me?" he asked out of nowhere.

My eyebrow went up. "I thought you didn't want it to become a regular thing with us."

"I don't," he said quickly. "We don't need it. Our sex life is great. Even better now for some reason, which I didn't think possible. I was just asking."

I knew him well enough to know he wasn't just asking. He had been thinking about it. "I think if the situation presented itself, we would talk it through, just like we did in Aruba. But I'm not going out looking for it. What about you?"

"Yeah, same," he said softly.

But I wanted to be clear with him. "Always be straight with me, Con. Did I wake a sleeping dragon? Is that what you want for us now? Tell me what you're thinking. I can handle it."

I felt Connor sigh against me, almost angrily. Before I could ask, he stood up and turned around. "I think I want to blow you right now."

I smiled. "Are you changing the subject?"

"Yes," said Connor. "I told you I don't need sexual freedom with other people. I just need you. Now you gonna let me suck your dick?"

I laughed. "You think I'm going to deny you that right?"

He got on his knees and pulled out my cock, which got hard the moment he told me what he wanted to do to me. He wasted no time: he deep-throated me, lips on my pubic hair, sliding up to the head, then went down again, making me moan out loud. He did it again and again, bobbed up and down, making small noises in his throat, his cheeks sucked in as his mouth enclosed tightly on me like a pump that was trying to get water out of an unused tap. My eyes rolled back as he kept the same steady rhythm, all mouth and no hands, as his thumbs were dug into the crease between my hip bone and groin. I started moaning his name over and over again, grasping what little hair he had and pulling hard. He didn't stop, didn't let up, until my cock head swelled in his mouth, then at the last moment, he pulled from me with a POP sound. I started shooting cum right up into his face. He grabbed my penis and pumped it with his hand tightly, directing it toward him. My body seized up from my toes to the top of my spine, and the only part of me moving was from Connor pumping more cum out onto his face until nothing was left.

He squeezed my dick hard as the last drops came out, then deep-throated one more time, slowly, no suction at all; it was just his warm, wet mouth and his lips all the way down, then all the way up. *Connor wins the gold, again.*

I fell backward on the steps, my cock still exposed, feeling like I just ran a marathon and had a heart attack at the finish line.

"Fuck baby … fuck…" was all I could get out in between breaths.

Connor put me back in my pajama pants and turned back around to sit between my legs, cum literally dripping off his dark blond eyebrows as he licked his lips. My cum slut baby started taking it off with his fingers and licking them.

Willy came outside just then, and I sat up. Connor looked at him nonchalantly with cum on his face but continued to suck his fingers. He walked past us, saying, "*Mi amigos, gracias* for putting on that show for me. I'm hard as a fucking rock. That was some amazing blowing skills you have there, Blue Boy. Now I see why you married him, Jamel, *de veras.*"

I laughed as he took the same path that Josh took, toward Nicky's gravesite.

CHAPTER 4

WHAT DO YOU KNOW?

Jamel

We got the call on New Year's Eve that Angie had the baby. So, two days later, instead of heading home from the airport, we went north to Boston to see their family, still in the hospital. We were in Connor's 4Runner, but I was driving because I hated the way he drove—too fast and like he wasn't afraid to die.

I heard Connor on the phone talking to Afia. "So, she's four months? Further along than Mina? Is that too far along to do something about it?" My ears perked up.

He listened, then said, "Wow. I'm kinda stunned. I mean … if that's what she wants to do. I guess I'm just trying to understand—" Afia must have cut him off and talked for a while because he just listened. Then he said, "You know you can tell me, right?" He smirked, then rolled his eyes. "Well next time we meet up, I'm going to get to the bottom of it." He listened some more, then giggled. Then they started talking about something else.

When he hung up, I asked, "So who's pregnant?"

"Winter. And this time she's keeping it. Can you believe that?"

My eyebrows went up. "Woooow."

"I know, right? And it's not Kevin's, so whatever rando out there she was fucking is about to get a big surprise."

My eyes got wide, but I kept them to the road. "Hmmmm…"

His eyes narrowed. "What do you know?"

I laughed. "What do I know about what?"

"Cut your shit, Jamel, I know you. You know something."

I laughed again. "I don't know anything."

"Uh-huh."

I shrugged. "We're here," I said, as I pulled into Mount Auburn Hospital's parking lot.

We stopped at the gift shop for presents for the new baby and took the elevator to her floor. As we were walking toward the room, Connor's father stepped out. He paused as soon as he saw us coming with bags of gifts for the family in our hands. Connor stopped walking too. They glared at each other with hatred, as they did in those very rare moments when they occupied the same space. Then Connor reached over and grabbed my hand. I wasn't sure if it was to show a united front, or he just needed my touch for security, but either way I held it tightly. Owen turned around and stepped back into the room.

"Fuck," Connor mumbled under his breath.

I knew there was no way he was going to go in the room with Owen in there. I was about to tell him that we'd come back another time when Owen stepped back out and walked in the opposite direction of us. I guess he was leaving so we could go in, which was completely surprising. For Evie's birth, he didn't. We came into the room, and he was sitting in a chair in the corner. He didn't talk but made Connor so uncomfortable by glaring at him that we didn't stay more than five minutes. I wondered if the old bigot had gotten softer over the years. Instead of a brick wall, he was shiplap.

Connor started walking but mumbled, "If Matty is in there, we're leaving."

"There is no way Matty is in there," I said to him. Angie spoke to Owen reluctantly because of their mother, but she cut Matty off completely after the trial, saying he didn't do the right thing when the time called for it. She has and always will be Connor's biggest ally.

We walked into a full room. Angie was sitting up in the bed with Evie on her lap, and Chad was holding his son. Chad was elated, his face glowing like he was the one who gave birth. If he wasn't the one making more money, I know he would happily quit his job and be a stay-at-home dad.

Lavell and Kendra were there with their girls. Vee saw us first and ran into my arms and squealed, "Uncle Mel!" Zee came right behind her, mimicking her older sister.

My mother-in-law was sitting on the edge of Angie's bed but stood up and hugged and kissed us both.

"Hi, Mom," said Connor and then made a beeline for the bathroom sink.

"Hello, Katherine," I said politely.

"Hello, Jamel," she said back just as politely.

I still call her Katherine, even though her other sons-in-law call her mom. I don't know why; she had accepted me in Connor's life since Connor came out and didn't treat me any differently, and she and my mama were super close. Maybe I still felt like it was a level of intimacy that we hadn't met yet, even after all these years. I mean, she hadn't exactly said to me, "Call me Mom" either, like I heard her say to Chad when he and Angie started dating.

"Where's Mary Kate?" Connor asked, as he washed his hands. I found a chair and started playing Patty Cake with my nieces, quietly waiting my turn to hold the newborn.

"She went to my house to grab clothes for Evie. She's going to take her for a few weeks so I can get settled with CJ."

"CJ?" Connor made a face of disgust. "You named that kid Chaaaad?"

"Chadwick Earl Worthington the Fourth actually. And shut up, your name is Connor, dude." I laughed at their usual banter on how Caucasian-sounding their names are.

"So another CH. E.W.?" Connor asked, as he came closer to Chad and the baby. "Give me Baby Chewy."

"Fuck off. Do not call my son Chewy!" Chad held the baby away from his brother-in-law.

"Language," Katherine said expectedly. "There are kids here, boys."

"Sorry Mom," they chorused.

Then Connor whispered, "C'mon, give me Baby Chewy."

Chad punched his arm playfully but then handed him the baby gently. Connor's face lit up, and he immediately started talking softly and whispering to him.

In these moments, I wish Connor would just relent and want to have a kid. Just one. He's so good with kids of all ages, from babies to teenagers. I know he would be such a great father.

But my thoughts were futile. I knew Owen fucked him up good, mentally, and ruined that part of him. Especially after knowing that, despite his older brother Matty going through the same physical abuse, he inflicted it on his own children, mostly his son Freddie. Matty may not hit him anymore, but he still puts him down a lot and made makes him feel like he isn't smart enough or good enough for anything. Connor believed in his heart he would be the same, hurting his own children in some way. *I wish he could see what I see. I wish he had more faith in himself.*

I turned away and noticed Katherine watching me watch Connor with the baby. She smiled at me, a little sadly. I must not have done a good job at hiding my feelings because I could tell she knew what I was just thinking. She reached out, and I took her hand and squeezed it.

Connor yelled, "C. Four!" We all looked at him. "He's Chad the Fourth, call him C. Four! Because he's going to be destroying shit all over your house."

Everyone laughed, including Chad. "C. Four. I like it!" he said happily.

Mary Kate and Dennis busted through the door, hand in hand. "We've made a decision!" She noticed us. "Oh, hi Mel, hi Connor. We made a decision, y'all!" she said again loudly, pulling Dennis with her. "Want to hear it!?"

"Sure, we do, Mary Kate. Let's make this day completely about you," Kendra said sarcastically, rolling her eyes.

MK glared at her. They were not friends at all, despite how close Kendra and Angie were. But Angie didn't like MK's pretentious best friend Candice either so that made them even.

Then she turned back to us. "We're going to be parents! We're going to adopt from the Philippines! We just did the application, and we have our introductory session tomorrow. Yay!"

"Yay!" Angie reached out from the bed with both arms and Evie mimicked her. MK went over and hugged them both, then Katherine started crying, making her daughters cry.

I reached over to give Dennis a handshake. "Congratulations."

Lavell and Chad came over and did the same. Connor handed the baby to me and came over to hug Dennis. They held each other tightly, and I could see Dennis holding back tears, sniffing every few moments.

"Thank you," he said quietly to Connor.

Connor patted his back. "That's what I'm here for," my husband replied.

❤

He didn't bring up the subject again until we were in bed. I thought he had fallen asleep next to me but then Connor said, "So what do you know, Mel?"

It took me a moment to figure out what he was talking about, then I laughed. "I said I don't know anything, Connor."

"See, I don't believe that," he said, and I laughed again. "I think you know something about Winter being pregnant. You spend more time in Providence than I do so you probably run into her." That really made me laugh out loud. "Seeee? Who did you see her with?"

I turned my body sideways to face him. "Like I said," I started as I touched his arm. "I don't *know* anything. But I was out having lunch with Ethan one day a few months back … and I saw her. With. Someone. Kissing. Someone."

His eyes went wide with intrigue. "Who?" he practically whispered.

"You're not going to believe me if I tell you," I sang to him. I moved closer and kissed his collarbone.

"I will if you tell me," he sang back, as he laid on his back.

"Weeeellll…" In between kisses all over his chest and abs, I told him, "Ethan and I saw Winter coming out of the back room of … Red Rock … after … kissing … BJ."

He balked and sat up. "Get the fuck outta here!" he yelled. I just looked at him. "You're shitting me!" he yelled again.

I fell backward laughing, and he jumped in my lap. "Are you for real? Are you fucking for real? You're not for real!" He bounced up and down on me like a kid making me laugh harder.

"I'm for real. Call Ethan right now," I said, laughing.

"Oh my God! Oh my fucking God! She's fucking BJ!! Hoooooly shit!!" He started bouncing on me again, while I cackled.

Connor kept yelling. "Do you have any IDEA how long BJ has been trying to fuck Winter? Like twenty years! And she never gave him the time of day. Not once. You want me to believe that not only is she fucking him, but she was fucking him raw!? And he got her pregnant!? And she's keeping Ben fucking Jenning's baby!? Holy fucking shit! I'm in the twilight zone!"

I couldn't stop laughing, especially since he was bouncing on my belly. "I can't confirm any of those things. All I said was that Ethan and I saw them kissing. Like, how you and I kiss. Like this." I pulled his face to me and put my tongue in his mouth.

"Mmmm." He moaned and slid down to position my penis between his ass cheeks, then started to grind back and forth on me, getting me hard.

"Do you think they did this too?" he asked on my lips.

"I don't know, let's try it and see."

I rubbed his perfect bottom and pulled his underwear all the way off, then I flipped him on his side and turned him around, moving my groin against his ass, kissing his neck and shoulder blades. I made my way down and licked his ass cheeks before my tongue found its way to his puckered hole. I tongue-kissed him there as he shivered and moaned loudly. He reached out and grabbed the lube off the nightstand and held it behind him. I took off my own boxer briefs, coated him and myself, moved his top leg to a 90-degree angle and buried myself deep inside of him. I leaned over and held his hand as I moved slowly in and out of him.

"Do you think they were doing it like this?" I said softly.

"Fuuuuck, Mel. If he was, I would be having his baby too," he moaned.

What the fuck did he just say!?

I stopped moving and looked down at him. He looked up and started giggling. "Don't fuck with me, Connor," I told him seriously.

"Okay, I'm sorry," he said sincerely. Then he said quietly, "Sometimes I think about it too. Days like today. I just … I just don't think I can." He looked at me with sad eyes. "Is that awful of me?"

I shook my head. "No, it's not awful. You're not awful. You're … human. If you feel like you can't, then you don't have to. I won't ever ask you so the decision will always be yours. Right now, the decision is we don't have kids and that's okay! Life for us is perfect as it is, and I don't really want to change it either. If you ever want to change that, you'll let me know. But I never want you to do something just because you think I want to do it."

"So, we didn't fuck Romy because I wanted to fuck him?" he asked me.

I looked at him like he was crazy. "Absolutely not. I wanted to fuck him too. He was fucking hot," I said and smiled.

He laughed out loud. We stared at each other, him looking into my gray eyes and me looking into his bright blue ones. Then he said to me, "How did I get so lucky?"

I started moving again. "Trust me, I'm the lucky one here."

I kissed and made love to my husband, pinching his nipples hard and stroking him from the front until he came in my hands, and I came inside of him. With his back against my chest and our bodies still connected, we fell asleep that way.

❤

Connor

Someone knocked on the manager's door. "Come in," I called from the desk.

My tenant, Nate Proctor, walked in with two little girls, one holding his hand and the other looking bored behind him. The smaller one was no older than Ethan's girls, around age eight, but the older one was about twelve.

"Hi, sorry to bother you but the thermostat in the second bedroom seems to be out. Can you come take a look at it or get someone in here quickly? I have my girls for the week."

"Sure, just fill out this form and I will get someone on it, tonight if I can," I said. "I B right?"

I hadn't had any encounters with him since he moved in about six months ago. I tried to introduce myself to him last August when I got back from Atlanta, but he just stared at me through a half-opened door, then grunted okay and closed it in my face. He barely spoke to me, which was fine; at least he knew where to go when something was wrong.

I put the work order form on the small round table in the office with a pen, and he sat down to fill it out. The smaller of the two girls walked up to my desk and pointed at the fake flowerpot of assorted lollipops sticking out. "Can I have one please?"

"Yes, as long as your dad says it's okay," I told her.

"It's fine," he said without looking up.

She grabbed a Tiger Pop, opened it, and put it in her mouth. She sat in the chair opposite my desk and said, "So what's your name?"

I sat on the side of my desk. "Connor. What's yours?"

"Leave the man alone, Lily," the older one said annoyedly.

"Shut up, Violet!" the one called Lily said back nastily.

"Don't tell your sister to shut up, Lily," Nate said lazily, again without looking up.

"Maybe you can offer your sister one?" I asked Lily. She gave me a dirty look, definitely the feistier one of the two.

Violet walked over and took a Blow Pop. "Thanks," she said. She sat down in the other chair.

"So, you're spending some time with your dad? That's nice," I said casually, trying to make conversation.

"Yes, we're Daddy's valentine this weekend because he doesn't have one," Lily said.

"Shut up," Violet said.

"Don't tell your sister to shut up, Vi," Nate said again lazily. I could tell this was a normal and repetitive statement.

"See, Mommy's valentine is Sherman, so she went away and left us with Daddy so he won't be lonely," Lily offered, more information than necessary.

Violet scoffed. "You talk too much."

Lily shrugged as Nate came over to hand me the paper. "You forgot to date it," I told him.

Lily asked, "Do you have a valentine?"

I laughed. "No, I don't. It's not something I celebrate."

I'd always felt it was just a reason to get laid and since I was getting laid on the regular, there was no reason to buy gifts for it. Jamel always felt it was commercialized and refused to spend money on that day. So, together, we ignored the holiday and celebrated what we called Half-Price Chocolate Day on February 15th instead.

Nate looked confused, as he tried to hand me back the paper he had just dated. "Yeah, you and your husband don't do anything for Valentine's Day?"

As soon as he said it, three things happened. My face went from a laughing smile for Lily to a frown for him, he immediately shut his mouth like he said too much, and I felt that feeling again, like someone who I barely knew knows too much about me. *So, what do you know about me?*

I didn't take the paper from him. Instead, I looked him in the eyes and asked him calmly, "How do you know I'm married?"

He looked up like he was thinking a bit, then said, "You must have mentioned it in passing."

Bullshit. "I don't think so, Nate."

"Well maybe I heard it from one of the neighbors," he mumbled. He tried to hand me the paper again.

Bull. Shit. "You heard from one of the residents that I was married? To a man?" I challenged him.

"I don't know, maybe," he mumbled again. He shook the paper at me to take. I took it from him as I held his gaze. Everything about this man suddenly made me feel uneasy. No, not uneasy. Rattled. And it had been a few months since I felt rattled like that.

"Thanks," he mumbled a third time and avoided my eyes. "Let's go girls, get to it," he said sternly, almost as if he was barking out orders, like he had been in the military or something.

I let him get as far as the door, then I asked him, "Hey Jarhead, where are you from again?"

He sighed, then turned all the way around and looked at me. "Connecticut."

Holy shit! Holy! Fucking! Shit! This asshole has been living in my building the whole time!?

I got a call last year when I was covering the Vet line for Taylor, a real piece of work who started out the conversation asking me personal questions and ended up calling me all kinds of gay slurs. I hung up on him, thinking it was some kinda prank call, but it really pissed me off. And now it appears Mr. L was right under my nose.

I was trying to remember if the call was before we went to Atlanta or Aruba, then remembered telling Ethan about him moving in the month of August. He already knew who I was when he moved here because he said he had seen me at the conference in New York and that was two years ago. He knew who I was when he made the call. *This sneaky sonofabitch!* He was lucky he had his two little girls with him. I would have knocked his fucking head off, as the anger burning in my chest was that great.

I slowly stood up and glared at him with my jaw tight, my eyes narrowed, and he stared back. He was holding onto Lily's hand again who wasn't paying attention, but Violet felt it.

She glanced back and forth between me and her dad. "What's wrong? What's happening? Dad?"

Nate relented first. "Nothing, honey," he called to her. He looked down at her and caressed her hair. He looked up at me again and said, "Thank you for your help. For my daughters."

Now if I was a petty asshole, I would have yelled out, "Oh, you need help from the dick-sucking faggot you cursed out a couple of months ago? Fuck that and fuck you!" But alas, I'm an adult with a full-time job with benefits, and an organization to represent professionally, so instead I said nothing.

He looked at me another moment, then said, "C'mon," ushering his daughters out in front of him.

I sat at my desk mad as fuck, trying to figure out what to do. *If I say something to Ethan, he's just going to offer to kick him out, which I shouldn't give a shit about but I do for some reason, two little ones that I just met in fact. If I say something to Jamel, he's just going to do that quiet talking shit and tell me to be rational but to keep an eye on him.*

I didn't know what made me think to call Jack, maybe because he'd been my fake therapist ever since he started his real therapy practice. I called his cell.

"Hey, Connor," he answered.

"What are you doing, man?"

"Working on a treatment plan. What's up?"

"You have a few minutes for me?"

"Always." I heard him shuffling around some papers. "What's wrong? You and Mel okay?"

"We're fine, this is something different. I need some advice." I told him first about the VVB call and then my new revelation.

He listened without commentary as he typically does, then asked, "What's your biggest fear right now?"

I scoffed. "My biggest fear is that he's a fucking stalker, and I'm going to find a dead bunny cooked in my backyard one day!"

"Connor, c'mon," he chided. "Do you really think he is stalking you? Because if you really think that, you should just call the police."

"I don't know, Jack," I said. "I don't know what he wants."

"So why don't you just ask him? Are you afraid of him?"

"Fuck no. We're about the same height and weight, but I would knock him out if he ever tried something with me."

"Okay," Jack said all calm, as if I had said I would invite him to tea. "So why not just talk to him, find out what he wants? Maybe he just wants to be friends."

"He told me he dreamed about me! Do you have sex dreams about your friends?"

"He said he dreamed about you, but didn't say it was a sex dream," Jack countered.

"He said it made him wonder if I was a top or a bottom."

"Yes, but that still doesn't mean it was a sex dream. It could just be about your masculinity; you don't present as gay at first glance. He could have just been curious about you *because* he dreamed about you, not the other way around. You might be who he wants to be—a Marine vet open about his sexuality."

"Calm down, *Jackie Bear,*" I teased him, "I don't want to be open about my sexuality with him."

He paused. "Don't call me that, asshole," Jack said, losing his therapeutic voice. I laughed. He hated when I called him by his pet name that only Ethan calls him. "Fuck you, I'm hanging up," he said.

"No! Okay sorry, damn!" He was quiet so I knew he was annoyed with me. "Dr. Frazier? Are you still there?" Jack was in the graduate program for his doctorate, but I called him that sometimes to boost his ego.

I heard him sigh. "Connor, I think you should talk to him first, then what he says will help you make a decision about what to do next. He called that day for a reason. Maybe he needed help and still does. Maybe he does have feelings for you. Maybe he just needs a mentor or a friend."

"Well fuck that, I won't be either of those things for him."

"That's understandable, and you can explain that to him. Either way you need to tell Ethan. Because if something were to happen in his building, he needs to know why."

Fuck, he was right. Hearing on the news that his building manager beat the shit out of a tenant was probably not how he would want to find out about all this. "And Jamel?"

"Is there a reason you wouldn't tell him?"

"He's just going to get upset. When the call happened, he all but threatened the guy, told me to tell him the next time he calls to put him on the phone. What is he going to do when he realizes the guy lives in my building?"

"He's going to be upset and be worried about you. Because that's what spouses do. But you should tell him, then together you will come up with practical solutions on how to handle it."

Fuck, he was right again. Jamel's not exactly the flipping out kinda guy; he barely raised his voice. But we'd also never been in a situation like this before and knowing him the way I did, this would piss him off. What he would do with it, I just didn't know.

"Okay, I'll tell Mel. And I will give Ethan a head's up, but after I talk to Nate. The kids are here for the next couple of days, but I will find him and talk to him sometime next week."

"That sounds like a good plan."

"Thanks, Jack."

"Anytime, man."

❤

I waited until we were settled at dinner, then said, "Hey, Mel? Remember that call I had a few months back, that L person?"

"Yeah?"

"I know who he is."

I told him what happened at work. He stopped eating and, just like he did when I told him about the call, his face became more stone-like. I also told him about the conversation I had with Jack and ended it with, "So I'm going to talk with him one day next week. See what his deal is. If he admits he came there just to get close to me, I'm going to break his lease and evict him. But if he denies and somehow convinces me he's not stalking me, then I'll just keep a close eye on him. I'm going to call Ethan tomorrow and tell him."

"No. You're going to call Ethan right now and tell him and then evict his ass tomorrow morning," he ordered me.

Sometimes I love when he gets all sergeant on me. Sometimes I need him to back off. This time it was the latter. "Jamel, let me handle it my way."

"No, fuck that. He's been stalking you since he saw you in New York. He's Googled you, found out about your life and us. This guy wants you and I don't know if it's sexual or admiration, but I don't fucking like it one bit."

"So if it is either of those things, do you think I can't handle it? I need Big Daddy to step in and take over?" I said sarcastically.

"Don't fucking do that, Connor," he said angrily. "This is your life we're talking about. Our life. If something were to happen to you, I would—" He closed his fist and couldn't get the words out. "Please just evict his ass and send him on his way. I don't trust him at all."

"I don't trust him either," I said back. "I would love to just send him on his way and be done with it, but I need to understand what this whole thing was really about. So let me do it my way. I can handle a homophobic asshole. Remember who my family members are."

"I am not okay with this," he said. "It's stupid and reckless. You want someone to talk to him, I'll talk to him, okay? I will handle this for you."

I was getting angry at how he was treating me. I really wanted to snap out and tell him to back the fuck off, but I felt like that would have just proved his point by coming off emotional and impulsive. So, I remembered The Major's words and took a page out of his book. I spoke calmly and put him in his place by saying what I needed to say and giving it to him straight.

"Jamel, I'm not your fucking wife. I'm your husband, and I'm a grown man. I can and will fight my own battles and I do not need you to protect me. You will stand down. I will handle it my way, and that's the end of it." Then I sat back in the chair.

He glared at me like he wanted to be the one to snap out, but we both knew he'd never do that. Instead he blew air through his nose roughly, got up, and went to the kitchen. He emptied his plate then started loading the dishwasher, banging dishes into the compartments. I gave him a moment, then I got up and went to stand behind him, and rubbed my fingertips up and down his back. He didn't acknowledge me at first.

"Mel?" I called his name softly.

He turned around and grabbed my face to kiss my lips forcefully. I let him, but then I pulled back and held his face too. I put my forehead on his and we stayed this way until he calmed down, and our breathing was in sync. He pulled me close with his arms around my neck and held me tight. I wrapped my arms around his body and held him tight too. We stood this way for a moment. He let me go first and looked at me, and I saw it in his eyes. He wasn't angry; he was worried. Scared a little. I understood him.

Jamel inhaled and exhaled slowly. Then said, "Okay."

"Thank you," I said.

He blew out air from his nose again. "Fuck!" he angrily exclaimed through his gritted teeth. Then he calmed down again.

I cocked my head to the side and said again, "Thank you."

He shook his head but pulled me close to him again. "You know I will kill him, right?" Jamel said into my neck.

I chuckled. "Yes, I know. And that's why I love you."

"Hmmm…" he hummed in my neck, then nibbled on it. Then he stepped back, pulled off his shirt and pulled me to the couch.

I didn't have to wait long. Ten minutes after I settled into the office two days later, Nate knocked on my door, then came in without my consent. I quickly stood up and glared at him.

"At ease, Jarhead, I just came to talk," he said, with his palms raised up.

I said one word: "Talk."

He sighed loudly, then motioned for me to sit down as he sat down in the chair his younger daughter occupied just a few days ago. When I did, Nate started with an apology.

"I'm sorry for the things I said to you over the phone. I was ... in a really bad place. That's not an excuse; it's an explanation. I called with the intention of getting help. But when you said your name ... I don't know ... it just triggered something in me. I was hurting and I wanted to hurt someone else. I'm really sorry about that."

It was definitely the same voice. How did I miss it all this time? "You said you had been trying to get me on the phone through the hotline. Why?" I asked him.

He swallowed like he had been caught. "After I moved in, I ... wanted to get to know you but ... I didn't know how to do it. I wanted to talk to you about ... what I was going through. I didn't think anyone else would understand. Being from a small town. Being a Marine. Being in the closet."

"I'm not in the closet."

"Maybe you're not anymore, but you were."

I sighed. "What do you want from me, L?" Then it hit me. "Oh! Nathani-EL. Got it." I gave him an OK sign with my fingers sarcastically.

He sighed again. "I don't want anything from you, Connor. Except I don't want you to kick me out. It's the first decent place I've lived in all year, and I don't want to lose it."

"Well, you should have thought about that before you stalked me, then disrespected me when I was trying to help you," I said flippantly.

"I didn't stalk you. I did see you in New York at a conference, but I did not plan on moving here because of you. I didn't even know you lived here in Rockville. I thought you lived in Providence. It was only when I got here to view the apartment that I realized you were the same person I saw two years ago, and that you had a real full-time job. I found this place on a website that was … accepting."

"Oh, so you're gay now?" I asked mockingly.

"I don't know what the fuck I am," he said seriously. "I should have taken you up on that offer to talk to someone, because I spiraled after that call. But I'm okay now. I have a therapist. I'm in AA, three months sober. I'm trying to get my life back in order. So please. I'm asking you. No, I'm begging you. Don't evict me."

Fuck. I hate this guy, but also I care about his fucking well-being. Ugh, I hate being like this.

I kept my face stoic and said, "I'm not going to break your lease. Just stay the fuck out of my way for as long as you're here."

He looked relieved. "Okay." He hesitated, then said, "Does your husband know about me?"

"Yes. All of it." I glared at him again.

His eyes widened in fear. "He's not going to come after me, right?"

I scoffed at him. "Why would you think he'd come after you?"

"I mean, he's a big, Black, meaty guy so—"

No really, fuck this dude! "Are you a racist, too? Get the fuck out of my office!" I yelled at him as I stood up.

"Fuck, I'm sorry; that came out wrong," he said as he stood up too. "I just meant—"

"I know what the fuck you meant. Big, Black men are prone to violence and scare you, I've heard it all. Except the big, Black, meaty guy doesn't get into fights,

I do. So, you should be more afraid of me, asshole. Now get the fuck out," I told him coldly.

Nate stood up and nodded at me. "Trust me, Connor. I am. For a lot of reasons."

I wasn't sure what that meant, but I sure as hell wasn't going to ask. He turned to walk out, then said, "Thanks. I mean it. And I really am sorry. I mean that too." Then he left.

I sat back in my chair and let all the air out of my lungs. I decided to tell Ethan I wasn't breaking his lease, but if I got one inkling he was coming after me, it was going to be a problem. His problem.

CHAPTER 5

YOU'RE THE LAST ONE, CONNOR

Connor

The only way I was going to get her to start talking was to corner her. So, I asked Jamel, Ty, and Sam to play Daddy Day Care at Afia's house and had my tribe over the following Saturday night at mine. We had mocktails because none of them could drink, being either pregnant or breastfeeding. Winter was definitely showing at six months, and Mina was right behind her at about four and half months. She hadn't bought any maternity clothes of her own so Afia bought a bag of hers that they could go through, and they played dress-up at my house. Somehow, we started trading old sex stories and the wild stuff we used to do and get into, laughing hysterically on the media room floor.

"Oh my God, we were crazy back then, weren't we?" Mina said, after telling her story of fucking two stepbrothers and getting them high enough to fuck each other.

"I guess our crazy days are officially over," Winter said. "Well, mine are." She rubbed her belly and sighed.

"Winter, why are you not telling us who it is? Do you think we're going to judge you?" Mina asked. Winter turned her face away and didn't respond. Mina stood up angrily. "When the *fuck* did we start keeping secrets from each other!? We never did that; we always told each other everything!"

"Not everything," Winter said quietly.

"Yeah, like what? Because you all know everything about me!"

"What happened when you left back in 2009, Mina? You, Henrietta, June, and Jack?" Winter asked her boldly. "Where did you go? What did you do?"

We all looked at her. It was something we all wanted to know for all these years and never spoke about.

She stuttered a bit. "I… I… It's not… You don't understand. If it was about *me*, I would tell you. But it wasn't about *me*." She sighed and sat down. "We went to help Jack … settle a score. To make sure he came back alive. And that's all I can tell you so please don't ask me what we did."

"Settled a score? That sounds like someone got wacked, Goodfellas style," I joked. She looked at me seriously. My mouth dropped and my eyes went wide. "Holy shit!"

"Don't you ever, ever mention it to him, Connor," Mina pleaded. "I know how close you two still are. Promise me."

"I promise!" I said quickly.

I had so many questions, but I knew none of them would be answered. And truthfully, I didn't want them answered; it was one less secret for me to keep. Afia had her hands over her mouth and her eyes wide. She and Jack were also still really close.

Winter asked the question floating around. She moved over to her and asked her quietly, "Did you kill someone, Wilhelmina?" We never used Mina's full name, but it seemed fitting right now.

She shook her head slowly. "*I* did not." She emphasized that it was not her.

I always knew Jack was a bit of a sociopath and probably capable of murder in the right circumstances, but to actually know that it happened was blowing my mind.

It was deadly quiet, and then Mina broke the silence. She looked around and said casually, "Well, that's my secret. Who else here is keeping secrets?"

No one spoke for a moment, still taking in the revelation that our friend was a killer. Then Winter, who was still looking at her, said, "Mina and I had full-blown lesbian sex back when we were like nineteen."

Mina yelled at her, "Fuck, Winter!"

That broke all the tension in the room. I started laughing loudly. I could tell that was not the secret she wanted to come out. She swung out and hit Winter on the arm.

Afia jumped up yelling, "I fucking knew it! I knew you were fucking around with each other."

"Oh, calm down; it was one time, and we were high and bored," Mina said dismissively. I was still stunned and laughing at their confession. I kinda knew it too.

Mina turned to me. "And what about you two, huh? You're still gonna act like y'all *neeeever* fucked? Ever?" She looked from me to Afia. My Lovie and I stared at each other. I was definitely not going to own up to it, so it was on her.

"Okay, okay." She sat down and didn't look at me as she spoke. "Remember how I told you that Raymond took my virginity? Well … he didn't." Then she took a sip of her drink and smirked. Both Mina and Winter's jaws dropped as I smiled.

"Shut the fuck up," Winter said in disbelief. She looked at me with her eyes narrowed and asked, "When?"

I knew what she was thinking. It was rumored that Afia and I were sleeping together when I was with Winter, but we assured her that wasn't the case. "Not when we were in high school, Win, I promise. I never lied to you about that."

"When?" she asked again.

"My prom night," Afia answered her. "When he came home with a pass from the Marines to take me to prom."

"Awww. That was sweet," Mina said smiling and Winter relaxed.

"It was sweet," Afia said laughing, and I started blushing.

"Just the one time?" Winter asked.

We looked at each other again. I answered with shrugged shoulders. "Maybe one other time after that. When I came home for good."

But she said, "Maybe twice in the same night." She smiled at me, making me smile and my face flushed pink.

"You could have told us, you know," said Mina. "We always knew that if Connor didn't like sucking cock so much, you would be together."

We all laughed. I said, "Fuck you, Mina; you like sucking cock just as much as I do."

"Well, I've only sucked one cock for the last six years so I guess my appetite has changed," she said and laughed.

Knowing that I had sucked another cock recently made me smile. I don't know what made me tell them, but I did. "Jamel and I had a threesome in Aruba."

All three screamed at me, "WHAT!?"

"Connor, how could you!" cried Afia.

"What makes you think it was my idea?" I looked at her surprised. "Because I will have you know, he brought it up first. After we met this guy who propositioned us. After we ended up accidentally in a sex club and I gave Mel a blow job in a crowd of people."

"What the fuck?" Winter said laughing.

"Okay, you know you have to tell us all the details!" Mina said gleefully.

"I'm not going into details," I said, secretively. "That's between me and my husband. I just didn't want to keep a secret from you all." I smiled slyly.

"Okay, just tell us one thing, no two things," Winter said, as she got closer to me. "Was the guy hot?"

I closed my eyes and said dreamily, "Soooo fucking hot."

That made them all cackle. She said, "Ooooh and two, how was it after all this time?"

"It was ... different. It felt weird being with someone else, then watching someone else get fucked by my husband. But it was exciting too because we did it together. We fucked him, *to-ge-ther* if you know what I mean." They started giggling. "That was the best part. Then I got high and don't remember the rest." I started laughing.

"Holy shit, Connor!" Mina squealed. "Will you do it again?"

"I don't know. Anyway, that's my secret," I said non-chalantly. "Who's next?" I looked at Winter, but Afia began to talk really fast.

"Ty and I go to strip clubs together, then fuck in back rooms."

We all turned to look at her wide-eyed. "I'm sorry, could you repeat that, Lovie?" I asked amusingly, holding my ear out.

"We got invited out to a male and female strip show in December, and we just weren't having a lot of passion for each other with three kids, so we went. And we liked it a lot. We got a hotel room that night and fucked like we used to do when we first got together, all lust and passion. So, a few weeks later, I got the idea to just go to a strip club. We went to a female one and went into the back room for a private show. He got a lap dance, and then we fucked right there in the room. The next month we went to a male one, same thing, I rode his dick in the chair. So … it's kind of our thing now. We went last week."

We all just stared at her, then started giggling. "See, this is why I didn't want to tell you!" she whined. "I knew you were just going to laugh at me."

"I promise you we aren't making fun of you, Lovie," I said as I laughed. "It's just that ... you've never done things like that before you were married and—"

"And now all of a sudden you're fucking in back rooms of strip clubs? Who the fuck are you!?" Mina yelled at her. We all started laughing again.

She shrugged, then laughed. "I learned from the best how to keep things spicy, I guess."

We were all laughing so hard, tears were rolling down our faces. When it died down, I looked at Winter again. I touched her leg. "We love you, Win. You can tell us."

She sighed and sat up in a kneeling position. "You really don't know, Connor? Jamel didn't tell you? Or Ethan? Because I know they saw us and pretended like they didn't."

I looked at her curiously. "Saw who ... where?" I would rather her tell us than let her know that I already knew.

She looked at me for a long moment. Then she turned to Mina. "And he hasn't told Sam yet?"

Mina's eyes went wide. "Who hasn't told Sam ... what are we talking about, Winter? It's someone we all know?"

She looked at her intently too. "If he didn't tell Sam, that means he hasn't told anyone all this time. He's waiting for me to decide. Or tell you first. Before he tells ... his brother."

I grinned.

Mina sat all the way up and grabbed her arms. "Nooooo," she said, stunned. Winter nodded yes.

"When. The fuck. Did you. Start sleeping. With Benjamin!?"

Winter cringed and said, "About a year ago now … I think…"

Mina screamed, "AND YOU NEVER FUCKING TOLD ME!?"

She started shaking her friend's arms, and Winter pulled out of her grip. "I'm sorry! I was kind of… the first time we were fucked up. But then we weren't fucked up, and I think I was just kind of … embarrassed that … I liked it. A lot." She cringed again.

"So, this is why you haven't been around?" Mina asked. "You've been avoiding BJ? Has he even seen you since last October?" Winter shook her head no. "I don't understand, are you together or not? Are you doing this alone?" She just kept shaking her head.

"Does he know!??" I asked.

"I don't know, I don't know," she kept repeating.

"Holy shit, Winter," I said, shocked. "You can't keep this from him. Do you love him or not?"

"No," she scoffed at me. "I mean … I don't know. How the fuck do you know if you love someone? We've never been on an actual date, and I'm having his fucking baby. This is not about love!"

"Then why?" I asked her. "Why are you having his baby?"

"I don't know," she wailed, as she sat back down. We all sat close to her. "He told me to do what I wanted: abortion, adoption, whatever I wanted to do. That it was completely my choice. But BJ is almost forty with no kids, and I just couldn't do that to him.

This is why you don't fuck your friends!" she whined, as we reached out and comforted her.

She was quiet for a moment, then said, "He never even questioned whether it was his. He knows I'm a fucking whore, and he had every right to ask me directly if it was his, but he didn't. He just said, 'Okay, what do you want to do?' I told him I would let him know and that was the last conversation we had. That was four months ago." She sniffed and let her tears flow.

Mina asked, "What do you want, Winter?"

"That's what I've been trying to get her to figure out," Afia said. "Because this baby is coming, and she has to figure out if she is doing it alone, or with him, or putting the baby up for adoption."

"I can't put his baby up for adoption. But I don't want to do it alone," she said quietly, as the tears came down her face.

"Then don't," I said. "Because everything that I know about BJ, that we all know, he won't let you do it alone; you just have to tell him. Because if you don't tell him, he's going to think you want to be a single parent."

"But I don't know if I want to be with him either."

"Figure all that out later," Afia said. "But for now, just tell him that you're still pregnant and planning on keeping the baby. Because I don't think he knows for sure what you're doing."

I stood up and made the decision. "Let's go. Right now. We'll go with you, all of us. Whatever he says, we'll be here for you. But we're doing this, and we're doing this now."

Afia stood up too. Then Mina. Winter wiped her face and stood up. I grabbed my keys, and we headed out.

The bar was crowded for a Saturday night. BJ hires bands from time to time, and it seems to draw out crowds like this one. When we got to the door, Winter tried to bail, saying, "I can't talk to him." But we held her arms firmly.

"Go big or go home," Mina said. "And you're not going home. So, get your ass in there."

We walked in together and stood near the entrance. I spotted him first and said to them, "Wait here."

I walked over to the bar as BJ was coming out of the back room with ice for the bin. "Hey Con, you need a table?"

"No, I need you." He looked at me strangely. "Winter is with us. She wants to talk to you."

His face went from confused to fearful. He leaned over the bar and asked me quietly, "She's still…" He looked at me. I nodded. His eyes lit up. Then he nodded. "I'll be right there."

He went into the back, and I walked back over to my tribe. Her face fell. "He's not coming," she said, defeated.

"No, he said he'll be right there," I told her.

We waited about five minutes, and then BJ came out from the back with a different shirt on and looked like he'd combed his hair and beard. I smiled at him as he walked over.

Mina stepped up to him first. "Remind me to beat the shit out of you for knocking up my best friend, okay?" She playfully punched his arm. He smiled at her, then she moved away.

Afia was next. "You better say all the right things, BJ," she said, scolding him like a parent would. "All of them." He nodded at her. She leaned up to kiss his cheek, then moved to the side to stand next to Mina.

I walked over to him and said, "I was really scared when I came out, first to my friends and then to my family. Both times you were there for me." I patted his chest. "Be that guy."

He squeezed my shoulder tightly, then nodded. I went to stand next to Afia and Mina and the three of us linked arms. It was just Winter left.

He walked up to her, and she shifted her feet and averted her eyes. He looked down at her stomach, then up to her face. He asked her plainly, "You're keeping it?" She nodded. "Okay," he said casually. "Just tell me what you need. Whatever you need, I'm going to do for you."

She said quietly, "I just don't want to do this alone. I don't know what that means for us, but I can't do this by myself."

"You won't," he said definitively. "You're not having a baby; *we're* having a baby, right?" She stared at him. He asked her, "So, are we having a baby?"

She looked up at him with tears in her eyes. "We're having a boy."

His mouth dropped. He hesitated but then gently touched her protruding belly. "A boy?"

She shrugged. "Ben Jennings Jr., Jr. I guess."

BJ gasped, looking at her shocked. He held his finger up and moved it around, saying, "I'm going to tell all these people, okay?"

She laughed and wiped her eyes. "Oh, I don't care anymore."

He stepped back and said, in his very loud voice, "Stop the music, STOP THE FUCKING MUSIC!"

Someone heard him, and it died down. He pulled a chair over, stood on it, and yelled, "This beautiful woman is having my baby! I'm having a boy y'all!"

Everyone started clapping, yelling, cheering, and hooting. He got off the chair and kissed Winter on the mouth, then her belly.

Sam ran over first, his mouth in a solid o. "What the entire fuck did I just miss!?" he yelled. Mina walked over to her husband and explained the birds and the bees to him.

Several people started coming around, giving them both handshakes and hugs. I was smiling widely and clapping too when my Lovie turned to me and said, "You're the last one, Connor."

She winked at me. I laughed, kissing her cheek.

CHAPTER 6

LIKE A FAMILY

Jamel

After I showered and got ready for a housing inspection in Pawtucket that March, I came out of the bedroom and noticed that the second bedroom door was closed. That meant that Freddie was in there. I quietly went to go check on him, and he was sound asleep. I looked at the time and noted that he was not going to school, not if he was there on a Wednesday morning. I sighed and debated waking him up and making him go. But then I realized that if he came to my house in the middle of the night, something must have happened, so I left it alone and quietly closed the door.

I went downstairs, made coffee and a bagel for myself, and pulled out the ground beef and potatoes to make burgers and homemade French fries for dinner. Connor was away in San Francisco with Taylor, doing a panel on the homelessness in the city where their part was particularly talking about the vet homeless population. Then they had some mixer tomorrow, specifically for gay vets and service men and women. They almost canceled it because of the global pandemic finally reaching the states and causing major issues, but San Fran was still considered relatively safe, compared to Los Angeles, at that time. Connor wouldn't be home until Friday, so it would be just Freddie and me. I wondered how long he would crash here.

As I was heading out the door, the garbage truck was passing by my house. Jon waved at me, and I waved back. When he walked back over from emptying the trash, he said to me, "I haven't seen you in a while, Jamel. I thought you might have moved out and moved on." He grinned at me.

True to his word, Connor took out all the garbage on Tuesday nights and liked to have his coffee on the front porch on Wednesday mornings. And whether the truck was there or not, he kissed me every morning on the front porch. Even though we had not talked about it, I knew that something about Jon made Connor feel like he had to stake his claim with me. I wasn't exactly flirting back, but maybe I did like the attention a little too much, and that was enough to make Connor feel threatened. I never wanted him to feel that way, so to put a stop to the flirting, if I heard the truck, I had been stalling leaving the house until the truck had passed to avoid having any encounters with Jon. But it slipped my mind that day, between the change in my routine with Connor not being here and Freddie showing up.

"Yeah, just been working, you know?" I said casually.

"Yeah," he said. "I see your boyfriend a lot though. I don't think he likes me."

I smiled internally. "Husband," I corrected him.

"Oh! I didn't see a ring, so I thought—"

I cut him off by holding up my left hand so he could get a closer look. "Ten years," I told him.

"Tattooed rings. That's cool." Jon dropped the bins and walked backward as the truck was leaving him behind, asking me with a smile on his face, "Is it a happy one though?"

I laughed at his persistence. "Yes. Very happy."

"Ooooh!" He pretended to grab his chest as if he was in pain, making me laugh again. "I had to shoot my shot, right?" Jon winked at me, then turned around, running to catch up to his truck. "Bye, Mel!" he yelled out.

"Bye, Jon," I said softly.

I was back from work by the afternoon, and Freddie was up, in the kitchen cutting up the potatoes for the French fries later. He pulled all the seasonings out onto the counter that I used for cooking. He liked that I seasoned mine with Adobo before putting them into the deep fryer.

"Hey, Uncle Mel!" My nephew greeted me happily, like he didn't just skip school and camp out at my house all day. "Are we doing these on the grill or on the stove?" he asked, pointing to the ground beef.

"We can grill if you want." I shrugged. I leaned on the fridge and watched him with my arms folded across my chest.

Freddie looked at me, then looked back down. "What?"

"You know what. What happened?" I asked.

He sighed. "I got into a fight with my dad. No biggie."

"Big enough for you to come all the way over here in the middle of the night." He didn't respond. "What happened, Freddie?"

He sighed again and stopped cutting. He turned around to face me and mimicked me with his arms crossed.

"He just said some real stupid, ignorant shit." He got quiet, and I waited for him to continue. "At dinner he was talking about Aunty MK, about how she isn't adopting white children but children from the Philippines. He said that Filipinos were the dirty Mexicans of Asia. So, I just reminded him that Aunty MK is the only one of his siblings who talks to him and if he wants that to keep happening, he should watch his fucking mouth."

He paused for a moment, and I was pretty sure he said it exactly like that to his father.

"So, he took off his tie, rolled up his sleeves, and came over to me. I thought he was just going to hit me so I also reminded him that he can't put his hands on me, or I'll tell Uncle Connor."

He paused again and looked away. Knowing Freddie, I was almost positive he said that real smugly to piss his father off, which made his father want to strike him.

"So, he wrapped his tie around my neck real tight and choked me with it, dragging me by my neck out of the chair into the living room."

I'm going to murder that sonofabitch.

Freddie touched his neck absentmindedly, and I noticed he had a red line around it with bleeding scratches, where he desperately tried to get the tie off him. I unraveled my arms and came closer, as he continued to talk while not looking at me.

"He choked me and said ... that I'm his stupid motherfucking kid, and he can do whatever the fuck he wants to me. That he could kill me if he wanted to. I thought he was going to ... I couldn't breathe ... but he let my neck go and kicked me a couple of times in the stomach and said, 'Now go tell your ... Uncle Connor that.'"

I held his chin gently and leaned Freddie's head from side to side to survey his neck, saying quietly, "He didn't call Connor's name."

"No. You know what he called him."

I nodded. I went to pull his shirt up to see the bruise that I knew was there, and he stopped me by holding the bottom of his shirt down. He looked up at me with the same brilliant blue eyes as Connor's, and I had the feeling of déjà vu. I had done this before, almost ten years ago, with Connor when I discovered his father was beating on him. Two things hit me: the burning rage that I felt back then, to go home, get my SIG, and put six slugs in Owen's chest was what I was feeling now, but it was toward Matty; and that Connor was going to want to do the same when he got home.

I said to Freddie, calmly and quietly, "Let me see."

He hesitated but then let the bottom of his shirt go. I lifted it up to see the huge, black-and-blue mark on the side of his body. I touched it, and he winced. I moved gentler, making sure no ribs were broken. They didn't appear to be. I pulled his shirt back down and pulled my nephew into a hug. Freddie didn't resist. He wrapped his arms around me and held me tighter, then he started crying.

He rubbed his tears and snot on my shirt and said, muffled, "I hate him. I wish you were my dad."

My heart melted for this kid of mine. "Me too, Freddie. But I'll be the next best thing, how about that?"

He nodded. I kissed the top of his head and said, "C'mon. I'll make sandwiches for lunch while you finish prepping the potatoes, and we'll grill the burgers outside later. Want bacon on it?"

Freddie looked up with teary eyes, smiling at me, and then nodded again.

After dinner, we were sitting around watching TV and eating ice cream when Connor texted me.

[Connor: Matty just called me. He asked where Freddie was. Is he there?]

[Jamel: Yes]

[Connor: He wants you to send him back home.]

[Jamel: No]

[Connor: Um … okay. What's up?]

[Jamel: We'll talk when you get back.]

[Connor: What happened?]

[Jamel: Not over the phone. I'll explain when you get back.]

[Connor: Did he put his hands on my nephew again!!!?]

[Jamel: When you get back. We'll talk.]

[Connor: I'm going to fucking kill him.]

[Jamel: Don't do anything impulsive. I've been resisting the urge to grab my friend and pay his dad a visit all day. I need you to be the calm one right now.]

[Connor: You sound upset.]

[Jamel: Thanks Captain Obvious.]

[Connor: LMAO! Okay I'll chill. But is he okay? How bad is it? Like before or worse?]

[Jamel: He's fine now. I got him. You'll see when you get here.]

[Connor: Thanks. And thanks for taking care of him. I know he could be a pain in the ass.]

[Jamel: He's my nephew too. Stop thanking me. I love him too.]

[Connor: I know you do. Like he was your own. Love you.]

[Jamel: Love you.]

I put my phone aside and said to Freddie, without looking at him, "You're staying here the rest of the week." He grinned. "I'm taking you to school in the morning." He frowned. "When the show goes off, go take your shower and get to bed."

He looked like he wanted to protest so I turned to him and gave him a stern look.

"Yes, Uncle Mel," he mumbled.

When Connor came back on Friday, he reacted exactly the way I expected: yelling, cursing, and threatening to inflict bodily harm on Matty . But I was a lot calmer, so I reminded him of the plan. I had already taken pictures of Freddie's bruise and neck, and I sent them to him. Connor forwarded the pictures to both Matty and Stephanie and said to them, in a text:

[Connor: That was two. The third one is going to the police and children's services. Keep your fucking hands off him. Period. And he's staying with me until the schools open again in two weeks. You have a problem with this, come find me.]

Little did we know two weeks would turn into five months.

The coronavirus hit Providence, not as hard as New York, but enough for the governor to shut shit down here too. Although Connor wasn't showing any symptoms, something told him to get tested, since he was in California, and he indeed tested positive for Covid-19. He was one of the lucky ones; he never got sick, except for a stupid runny nose. Nevertheless, we quarantined him to the basement for fourteen days, which almost killed my sexually insatiable husband, not being able to touch me. But because of Matty's cancer diagnosis, Stephanie told us to keep Freddie longer just in case he had it too. She sent Freddie's clothes and laptop so he could do remote learning and schoolwork with us.

Then in the second week of April, EJ showed up at our door one night, asking if he could stay. Apparently, he got into a fight with his father too, a verbal one because as much as Ethan threatened to me that he'd knock EJ out, he would never actually put his hands on any of his children. I texted Ethan to let him know that EJ was there. He sent back two words:

[E: Keep him.]

When I showed Connor the text, he looked at me, stunned, and asked, "When did we become the home for wayward boys? What the fuck is going on in this world?"

We let him stay the night, then I went over to his house in the morning to talk to his father. I stayed near the car, and Ethan came out on the porch to talk to me. "Hey. I know you got Freddie over there so if you need EJ to come home, just bring him back."

"EJ's fine; we have the room," I said. "What happened? All he said to me is that his father hates him."

Ethan sighed and sat down on the top steps. "I said some shit that I shouldn't have said. But fuck, he makes me so mad all the fucking time. I don't know what to do anymore."

I leaned on my car door and folded my arms. "What did you say?"

He sighed again. "This whole 'I'm not gay' shit is annoying. He says it at the stupidest times. We were eating dinner, and the girls were talking about some show and JC said a lot of the stars on the show are gay, and he just yelled at her that he doesn't care, that he's not gay. So, I'm like, 'Ay yo, don't yell at your sister over this dumb shit. Nobody said you were gay. Nobody cares if you're gay or not.' He starts yelling at me, saying how I want him to be gay, that I want him to be just like me, but he is nothing like me." He scoffed.

"Did that hurt your feelings?" I asked him gently.

He scoffed again. Then said quietly, "Maybe a little. Maybe that's why I snapped at him."

I nodded. "What did you say?" I asked again.

"I don't remember everything; we just said a lot of nasty things to each other. But then he said that he wished I would have left him with his mother. That a pill-popping drug addict for a mother was more acceptable than a gay father. What kind of shit is that?"

"Ouch." *I'm going to have to have a talk with him, too.*

He continued. "So, I told him…" He blew out air loudly. "I told him that I didn't have a choice. That she didn't want him and left him with me so to suck that shit up because I'm all he's got."

I groaned. "Ooooh, Ethan."

"I know, I knoooow," he groaned too. "As soon as I said it, I regretted it. His face went from hurt to complete rage. He screamed at me that he hated me and fuck me and all kinds of fuck off, then left the house, got on his bike, and took off. I figured he was going to Freddie's house or Imani's house. I didn't realize Freddie was still with you."

"Fuck." I shook my head. "I'm gonna let him stay a few days to cool off if that's okay."

"Yeah, it's fine by me." He sighed, lost in thought.

"Where was Jack in all this?" I asked.

Ethan laughed bitterly. "Jack was trying to calm it down for both of us but after I said what I said, he turned on me. When EJ ran out, he got up to go after him, and I kind of snapped at him too. Told to leave him out there. We started arguing and … fuck, my mouth was just fucking shit up everywhere yesterday."

"Oh no. What did you say this time?"

He sighed for the fourth time and said, "I told him that EJ is my son, not his, and I'll decide how we handle him. Then I told him to sit the fuck down."

My eyes went wide. "Fuck, Ethan!"

"I know! I know!" he exclaimed. "God, the look Jack gave me could have killed me." He put his hands over his face.

"What did Jack do?" I asked. Because we all knew Jack had a bad temper and I wouldn't be surprised at all if he had hit him. Jack had been raising EJ with Ethan since he was two years old, and he loved that boy fiercely. Everything Ethan said and did was way out of line and extremely hurtful to both of them.

"Well, if the kids weren't there, I'm pretty sure he would have punched me in the mouth," Ethan said, confirming my thoughts. "But instead, he told me that all four of our kids, EJ included, were his goddamn kids and if I ever spoke to him like that again, especially in front of his goddamn kids, he would take all four of his goddamn kids and leave my ass. Then he left and went out looking for EJ. When you texted me, I texted him to tell him where EJ was, and he told me to fuck off." He sighed. "He slept in EJ's room in the basement; that's how far away he wanted to be from me. Then he got up early this morning, packed his kids up, and went to his parents' farm. So apparently, I'm on tim-eout from everyone." He laid down on his porch, with his knees up and one arm over his eyes.

I shook my head. "Is he coming back?"

"I don't know." Ethan looked at me and asked, "Would you?"

"Fuck no!" I yelled at him. "Shit, Ethan, go apologize to your husband for being a dickhead!"

"I am! I will. I just ... need to cool off too. I'm just so stressed out right now. This fucking 'Rona, man. It's just fucking everything up."

I sighed with him this time because I knew how he felt. I wasn't working because all non-essential work had been shut down, and all my guys were out of work too. Connor and I were basically living off our military pensions. He was still working for Ethan because the building still needed to be managed, but he told me Ethan waived April's rent for everyone there because he felt it was the right thing to do. However, the B&B had to close so he was just bleeding money. Jack was still doing telehealth therapy sessions so that helped. And thankfully they bought their home outright two years ago, so they didn't have a mortgage. Ethan, a successful businessman, had never been hard up for money but still, it was six mouths to feed in that house.

"I know," I said. "Maybe everything will get back to normal by May. Doubt it though."

"Well, whenever it does, I'm going to finally close on this small apartment building in East Greenwich that I want you to inspect for me and give me a quote on the renovations."

I threw my palms up in astonishment. "You just want me to give you a quote or are you giving me the job?"

"Well, you know, I gotta compare companies, see what's out there," he said smugly.

"Fuck you, asshole," I said, as I got back in the car, and he laughed. "Go apologize to your husband. In front of Jackie, Susie, and Jamie, since you thought it was a good idea to talk to your partner like that in front of *his* goddamn kids."

"I will."

"And send Jack by with some clothes. EJ is not going to want to see you just yet."

"Yep."

My friend laid across his porch, looking defeated. I told him one more thing. "And don't beat yourself up too much. Hurt people hurt people. You got hurt so you lashed out to hurt him back. But you forgot that you are the adult here, and he's the emotional child, not you. You fucked up. Now make it right."

He didn't say anything, but I didn't expect him to. I drove off, leaving him to think. I got about five minutes down the road when my text message alert went off with one word from him:

[E: Thanks.]

♥

So, for one month, we went from it just being Connor and I to a family of four. Connor woke them up in the morning and made sure they brushed their teeth and got ready for school before he went to work. I did the school stuff with them, making sure they sat at the dining room table and paid attention to the live virtual lessons, then actually completed the daily work. The phones were shut down between 9 a.m. and 3 p.m., and they were not allowed on any social media platforms during the school day, which neither of them was happy about. When they complained, I calmly let them know that at any point, they were welcomed to leave and go back to their respective fathers, and that shut them both up.

The gyms were closed so I got up at dawn and worked out every morning in the backyard. I cooked all the meals, since I wasn't working, and we had dinner together every evening and took the dogs for their walk afterward for some exercise. Connor took the nighttime routine too, making sure they took their showers and were in bed by 9 p.m. every night, and lights out by 10 p.m. On the weekends, we let them do what they wanted as long as they were safe, had masks, and carried hand sanitizer. Sunday nights were dinner and movie nights, and it was mandatory, our way of making sure they were home. But we let them pick the movies, no matter how much Connor and I hated the *Fast and Furious* franchise.

Jack joined us on Sunday nights. He forgave Ethan the next day after their fight when Ethan took my advice and humbly apologized in front of their kids and Jack's parents. But Jack left Ethan on timeout for five more days while staying at his parents' farmhouse with the kids, and he told Ethan's mother, so Ethan got an earful from her too. But every Sunday that EJ was with us, Jack had dinner here instead of with his family and stayed for movie nights. I know it was to make sure EJ knew he was loved and wanted by him.

Four weekends in, Ethan tried to do the same, leaving the kids with his in-laws and coming over for movie night. But EJ locked himself in the bedroom and refused to come out, so he left. After his father did, I knocked on the door.

"Let me in, EJ." He opened the door for me, then plopped back on the bed. "C'mon Ethan," I said, using his name. "You can't be mad at your dad forever."

"Don't call me that," he told me. "When I grow up, I'm changing my name. I don't want anything to do with him."

I sat on the edge of the bed and said, "Why? What is so bad about being Ethan's son?" He glared at me. "No really, I want to know. Because I'm gay, and if I ever had a kid, I would want to know how he really felt about me."

"It's not because he's gay," EJ whined.

"Well, that's what you told him."

"Well, that's not it!" he said angrily at me.

"Then what?" I asked calmly. He didn't respond. "Because from where I'm standing, I see a loving, committed, protective, sometimes overreacting dad who loves you so much. Who sometimes says stupid shit when he is hurt or frustrated or sad. And I see a kid in front of me that does the same thing." I waited.

"It's just… He doesn't understand me. He doesn't know how hard everything is for me. I'm so tired of everyone thinking I'm gay, just because my father is gay, and we have the same name."

"But you keep saying 'everyone.' Who is everyone? Two asshole kids at your school? C'mon it has to be more than that." He didn't say anything, so I asked the question.

"Do you think you might be into boys?" I asked him quietly.

"No!" he said automatically. "I like Imani. I'm into girls."

I nodded. "Okay."

EJ sat up on the bed and looked down at his fingers. "But … what if one day I start to … like … have feelings for boys? I don't want to be gay."

"Well, if you like girls and you start to notice boys, then that would make you bisexual or sexually fluid. Not exactly gay," I told him.

"But I don't want that either!" he yelled at me. "I just want to be normal! Nothing about my life is normal! Especially not my gay dads!" he cried.

Being that I am a proud gay man, that kind of stung a bit. I have normalized my sexuality since I was a teen, but knowing that I was on the outskirts of what was considered normal still fucked with me sometimes. But I pushed my feelings aside and said to him, "Your dads are normal, and so are you. Loving someone, whether they are the same sex or opposite sex of you, is normal, because love is normal. And whoever or however you end up loving someone is going to be just as normal. But you are fourteen years old and do not have to figure out any of this right now. So how about you just focus on being a kid named EJ before you start taking Kinsey scales?"

He looked at me curiously. "What's that?"

"Google it. In the meantime, can you please talk to your father? Apologize for the mean things you said to him? Let him apologize to you? Because as much as I love having you here, kid, your father loves you a hell of a lot more and wants you to come home. Your sisters and your baby brother miss you. Your Pops comes over every week just to see you because he misses you."

He didn't talk for a moment. Then he asked, in an incredibly sad voice, "She doesn't miss me. She didn't even want me. Why didn't she want me?"

I pulled him closer and ran my hands through his hair, as tears fell out of his eyes. "I don't know, EJ. Maybe your dad can answer that for you if you ask him. But I'll tell you this, she really fucked up not having you in her life. Because you are one awesome kid. You're funny, you're smart, you're kind, you're thoughtful, you're caring. You're everything I would want in a son. So maybe I'm a little jealous that my two friends have a kid as amazing as you. My two, *normal*, gay friends."

He smiled a little. "Thanks, Uncle Mel."

I called Ethan and told him to come back. We left Ethan and EJ in the basement to talk out their issues, and he stayed the night. In the morning, EJ went home with his father. But EJ was there the whole time we had Freddie and spent every weekend and most nights with us, so it was kind of like he never left.

We got a real taste of what it would be like parenting a smart-mouthed, oppositional, pain-in-the-ass teenager, and it challenged Connor the most, because like I've always known, they were just alike. They argued a lot, and Connor hated the back-talking that Freddie would do on the regular, and honestly, I did too. It was never just a "yes" or "no" with him; it was always a whine and complain, then begrudgingly doing what he was told. It came to a head one night in May when we had gone a few days without being intimate, and we obviously couldn't just send Freddie somewhere.

So, Connor asked him politely at dinner, "Hey, do you mind sleeping in the media room tonight?"

"Why?" he asked curiously.

"Because I'm asking you to," Connor replied.

"But why? Why can't I sleep in my room?"

"Why is this a big deal to you?" Connor asked, frustrated with him already. Freddie had spent plenty of weekend nights in the media room, falling asleep on the couch while watching TV and we let him, but because Connor specifically asked him to, all of a sudden it was an issue.

He shrugged. "Because I want to sleep in my bed tonight."

"Well, I'm asking you to do me this favor and sleep downstairs. Jamel and I want some privacy."

He smirked. "Why, so you can *fuck*?"

I tried to save him. "Freddie, don't be ru—"

"It's none of your fucking business why I asked," Connor snapped. "You don't get to ask me questions about what I'm doing in my fucking house. And because you want to be a smart ass, now instead of a request, it's a punishment. Now I'm giving you a direct order so go get your shit and take it downstairs to the media room, because that's where you're sleeping tonight!"

Freddie scoffed and stood up so fast, the chair fell to the floor. He looked exactly how Connor looked in Nick's house last year when he was frustrated with Henry and I.

"Alright already, fuck!" Freddie yelled and stomped upstairs with his fist balled in anger, then slammed his door.

Connor sat there for a moment, then turned to me and said, "If I did that to Owen when I was his age, he would have beat the ever-living shit out of me with his bare hands."

I nodded. My father mostly left the physical disciplining to my mama, but she sure knew how to wield a switch when we gave her back-talk. Even still, we wouldn't dream of ever yelling at my father. We just respected him too much.

"But you're not your father," I challenged him. "So, what are you going to do?"

I was willing to step in, but I felt like Connor needed to prove to himself that he could discipline this kid without violence.

He took a deep breath and went to the bottom of the stairs. "Fred. Come back downstairs," he called up to him.

Freddie opened the door and came to the top of the stairs, glaring at him. Connor said calmly, "You're going to come back downstairs and sit at the table again. You're going to apologize to Mel for that bullshit you just pulled. Then you're going to calmly get up, get your shit, take it downstairs to the media room, and that's where you're going to sleep tonight. And you're going to do it all respectfully. Because we don't deserve that type of disrespect from you. Not after all we've done for you."

Connor stepped to the side and waited. Freddie was quiet so I knew he was taking in Connor's words.

But he did it: he came back downstairs, picked up the chair, and sat in it. I sat back and watched him, and we waited for him to speak. He rolled his eyes, then sighed and looked upward. "Sorry."

"Nope," I said back. "Sit up straight and look me in the eyes when you speak to me."

He sat up in his chair and looked at me. "I'm sorry, Uncle Mel."

"For what?" I asked him.

He sighed again. "For being disrespectful."

I nodded. "Apology accepted. But there will be consequences. Now do what your uncle told you to do."

Freddie's face scrunched up. "What kind of—"

I put my palm out to stop him and said sternly, "You don't get to talk. You've done enough talking tonight. You have five minutes to go get your pajamas and your toothbrush, then take your shower downstairs and go to bed. Your night is over."

He looked like he wanted to slam his chair to the floor again, but I gave him the look my mama would give me, the one that said, "You try me and see what happens." He swallowed his words and got up, then went back upstairs without stomping. Connor sat at the table again and neither of us spoke. We waited until Freddie came back downstairs with his stuff in his hands.

He mumbled as he walked to the basement stairs, "I'm sorry, Uncle Connor."

"You should be," Connor said. "That stunt you pulled cost you the TV for two nights. You'll be sleeping in the media room without media. And I swear if you open your mouth, you'll be quarantined there for the next two weeks without it. I dare you to test me."

Freddie breathed out roughly through his nose, but he went quietly. As soon as I heard the door close downstairs, I smiled at my husband. "Good job, Dad." He glared at me.

Our instant family continued from the spring into the summer of 2020. We watched the entire video of George Floyd's death, and that was hard for all of us. We cried together, then decided to join in the protests. The four of us went to Black Lives Matter rallies in Providence, wearing masks, with our fists high in the air, Connor and I holding hands the whole time. But the best one was the vigil in Rockville at Wincheck Pond, led by Father O'Donnell, Connor's old priest at St. Cecilia's, and Pastor Lawson, from Immanuel Grace Lutheran Church. Apparently, Rockville had two churches, so you were either Catholic or Lutheran Protestant, and this was the first time in the history of Rockville that the two congregations came together. Everyone was to bring a candle, even the children, and for eight minutes and forty-six seconds, we were to either stand, kneel, or lay prostrated on the floor and say, "Black lives matter." The entire Rockville police force quietly joined us, kneeling in the background. Jack, Ethan, and their children were there as well, sitting in a circle holding candles, real ones for the adults and battery-operated ones for their three kids. EJ left us to sit with them.

Connor, Freddie, and I stood. I started repeating the mantra but after a while, I couldn't anymore. It just hit too close to home for me. Connor knew that being Black trumps being gay when it came to discrimination for me. My masculinity could hide the fact that I'm gay if I wanted it to; most people assumed I was straight, and it never came up in my line of work, but obviously I couldn't hide my skin color. So, if I was working late in a Caucasian neighborhood that I'd never been to, Connor would call me just to keep me on the phone until he knew I was okay. When we looked up places to visit for vacation, we made sure that they were gay-friendly and diverse. If we were out to dinner at an expensive restaurant, and the waiter purposely slid the check to Connor, he would smile smugly and slide the check to me. We didn't talk about why he did those things; he just did it, and I loved him for it.

After we bought the house and got the dogs, I walked them around the neighborhood by myself and got looks, not of curiosity but of fear. So, I only did it with Connor or he did it alone. It's been nine years, and I still don't walk the dogs by myself. I greet my neighbors no matter how I am feeling that day, and he knows why. I don't typically let him speak for me. I am able to be articulate on my own and keep calm in all situations, as my father taught me, but he has grown perceptive over the years and is quick to either step in or get us out of there when an encounter is starting to take an ugly turn with racial overtones. We haven't had anything overtly bad happen to us since our earlier days of dating, but we stay aware and vigilant because we have to.

We are a gay, interracial couple. And it's exhausting.

I listened to the two of them chant softly and with conviction, and the low murmur through the crowd as people chanted quietly to themselves led me to tears before I could stop it. Connor didn't stop chanting when he looked over at me. We locked eyes, and tears started falling out of his eyes as well, because he knew how I was feeling. And I knew he got scared for me sometimes. My greatest fear, that I inadvertently made his fear over the years, was to die at the hands of the police. Seeing George die that way, it hit me hard. And Connor got it, got me. He wiped my tears and wrapped his arms around me. We leaned on each other long after the chanting stopped, and there was just a hush over the crowd.

I don't know if it changed anything in their small town, but if one mind was changed that night, then it was worth it.

Once school was out, the boys convinced us to buy an above ground pool, an 18-foot by 48-inch monster that they loved. We hated it at first because our water bill went through the roof, but Connor and I quickly forgave them once we started having midnight romps after the kids went to bed. In June, we spent Father's Day all together at Ethan's house, as Freddie refused to go to his family's Father's Day Sunday dinner at Owen's house. And by July, Covid-19 cases were going down in our area so the nine of us spent Connor's birthday at our house, just our two families in person with a virtual party so others could join in, like his sisters, my brothers and Afia, Josh and Willy, and Henry's family. Winter and Mina also joined us via Zoom. They were sheltering in place at BJ's house with Sam and their new babies, born in May and June respectively.

My hair grew about three inches above my head, soft and curly like my mama's. I grew a full beard and a mini afro. My hair typically grew fast, and I never liked the "pretty boy" look on me, so I've always kept my hair cut short, unlike all three of my brothers who embrace it. My husband loved it because he had never seen me with hair, and it gave him something to hold onto when we made love. Connor let his hair grow out, long enough to tuck it behind his ears, but continued to shave until I told him his stubble was coming in sexy, then he let it grow out more. Both boys grew out shaggy looks, with Freddie's straight blond hair naturally falling more layered and EJ's hair with a bit more wave to it falling over his eyes like his dad's.

We stayed this way until the end of July when Ty and Afia chanced it, coming over with scissors and clippers and taking turns getting the four of us back to looking civilized. They brought Kim and Imani with them, which made our pseudo-sons very happy. Then Ethan closed on the apartment building in East Greenwich, and suddenly my team was back to work, finishing up the project we started back in March and working on the new one for Ethan at the same time. No one minded the long hours and extra work.

In August, Matty started asking, then demanding that Freddie return home or he would come over with the police, drag him out of the house, and arrest us for kidnapping. Freddie yelled, cried, and screamed about it, but we had to let him go when his father actually showed up at our house. Connor, of course, did not let him in, so he stayed in his truck and said Freddie had thirty minutes to pack up his stuff and come out or he was calling the police.

I could tell it was killing Connor to do so, but he helped Freddie pack up his clothes and school materials and told him what he always tells him, "Don't hesitate to come here, anytime, day or night. I will always be here for you. Especially if he is hurting you. No matter what he says or does, you find your way here."

And Freddie said to Connor what he told me, "I wish you two were my dads. EJ has no idea how lucky he has it."

We walked him out together. Freddie took one look at his father's car and grabbed my arm, looking up at me with sad eyes. I pulled him in for a hug, and he held me tight. "I'll see you soon, son," I said to him. He pulled back, and I touched his shoulder, saying, "Remember, I'm the next best thing." I winked at him.

He smiled and said, "Love you, Uncle Mel."

"Love you back, Fred."

I stayed at the top of the porch stairs while Connor led Freddie to the car. "Can I come here next Saturday?" Freddie asked desperately.

"Boy, what did I just tell you?" Connor playfully scolded him, lightly hitting him upside the head.

Freddie smiled and then embraced him. "Love you, Uncle Con."

His asshole father got out of the car and said, "Alright, alright, get the fuck in the car. And you better not be a fucking fag after spending all summer with these two." He looked up at me and gave me a dirty look. I smiled and gave him the finger.

Connor got in his brother's face and said, "Just give me a reason, Matty. Give me a reason to take your son from you. Because the next time you put your hands on this kid, he's staying here for good."

"Fuck off, nobody is putting a teenage boy in a home with two homos," Matty said nastily, as he pushed Freddie toward the car.

"Then I guess I'll just have to kill you and take him for myself," Connor told Matty with a straight face. Matty turned around and glared at him. Freddie smiled widely behind his back.

"We're still headed to Georgia next Thursday, right?" Connor asked, as we laid together that night. We had planned on taking Freddie with us on the drive and were disappointed that it wasn't happening now. We were looking forward to it as a family.

"Yup," I said, yawning. "Just in and out, like we planned. Atlanta is like a hotspot for Covid right now. But Josh wants us to come together on the anniversary for Nicky. Watch the sun rise. So we should be there in person. Plus, he finally bought those chickens so I would love to see him and Willy playing Old McDonald for a while."

He chuckled, then got quiet. I could tell he was thoughtful, but I wasn't sure about what. Then he said to me, "It's too quiet."

I laughed loudly. *Look who's missing the kids?* "Well, you know how we could change that, right?"

"Uuuuugggh!" he groaned, and I laughed again.

"Come on. Admit you loved it. You loved our little family. You loved playing dad for a while. You loved having a house with kids." I nudged him playfully.

He didn't answer for a long while. Then he said, "But if something were to happen and we had to take Freddie, you'd be okay with that, right?"

"You already know the answer to that, Con."

He got on top of me and started moving his groin against mine. "Our sex life took a real nosedive these last couple of months. You sure you want that?"

I held onto his butt cheeks and let him grind on me. "Because we went from every other day to just a few times a week? Or because you couldn't be as loud as you wanted?"

He pinched my nipple and laughed. "Shut up. And it was more like once a week."

I laughed. "There are some married couples with children who have sex once or twice a month."

"And those people suck," he said, making me laugh again. "We will never be like them."

"Then what would we be like?" I asked him.

He stopped grinding on me and said, "Like it was. Doing stuff together. Like a family."

I started tickling him. "Whaaaaat? Did Connor Adrian McIntyre just use the F word?"

"Aw fuck!" He giggled that silly laugh that I love and tried to move away from my fingers, but I held onto him with one hand and tickled his sides, laughing with him.

When the laughter died down, we stared at each other. I thought he was going to say something else about us having a family together but instead he said, "Make love to me."

Which meant he was getting too emotional and didn't want to think about this anymore. I pulled his body toward me, and we kissed, slowly and sensually. I rolled him over to his stomach and kissed him from his neck to his calves, pulling down his underwear and rimming him nice and slow. After I prepared us both, I turned him back over and entered him face forward. We kissed and touched and made love for a while, silently, lovingly.

CHAPTER 7

I'M SORRY FOR YOUR LOSS

Connor

I dreamed of Vinnie that morning. The last time I dreamed of him was the night Mel and I had our wedding ceremony two years ago. It started out like a memory, us sitting on the stone wall that we used to sit on all the time to trade cigarettes and talk shit. But he slipped something new in. He said, in his Texas twang, "You're already free, birdie. I took the lid off you a long time ago; you just needed someone to show you how to fly. So don't be afraid to fly." Vinnie had never called me "birdie" before, so I knew it was a sign. When Nick showed up at our wedding, I remembered his whole free bird status, and it made me smile. It was Vinnie reminding me that the only thing holding me back from finding love and happiness was me.

But this morning wasn't a memory at all. I dreamed that I was lying on the grass on the training field, waiting for the sun to rise. I looked to my right and expected to see Taylor holding my hand, but it was Vinnie. He was singing to me. The melody was familiar, but I couldn't hear his voice, couldn't make out the words. Vinnie and I never sang to each other, so it was weird. I had just figured out what song he was singing when my cell phone rang, cutting into my dream completely and I lost it.

I moved away from Jamel to look at it. It was Mary Kate calling me at 4 a.m., which never happens, so I answered, "What's wrong?"

She was crying. "Connor, he's gone. Dad ... he's ... it's almost over. Nobody wanted to call you, but I wanted you to know—"

"Slow down, what are you saying? What's happening?" I sat up.

Jamel turned over to look at me. Mary Kate took some breaths and said, "Dad had a stroke earlier this evening. He's brain dead and on life support. Mom didn't call any of us until it was too late. She called Matty, and Matty called me, and I called Angie. We drove down together; we're in Providence." She paused to cry a bit. "They are going to pull the plug soon. But there's still time. If you wanted to ... to say goodbye."

I wish I could say that I felt something for the old man at that moment. But the only thing that washed over me was overwhelming relief. *It would finally be over.*

"Thanks, Mini Kat," I said sincerely. "Do what you need to do. I'll say my goodbye from here." Jamel sat all the way up and touched my arm.

She sniffed a few more times. "Okay. Father O'Donnell is here. We're going to say a prayer and then head back home. But Angie and I are packing clothes and coming back to the house later on today to stay with Mom until after the funeral. I don't want her to be alone. She's all alone now." MK started crying again. "Will you come too?"

"Of course. Tell Mom I'll stop by in a few hours."

"I can't believe this is happening. It doesn't feel real, does it?"

"No. No it doesn't. I'm gonna go. Hug and kiss Mom and Angie for me." I hung up before she said anything else.

Jamel leaned into me. "Who?"

"Owen," I said without looking at him. "They are pulling the plug now. He's dead."

I leaned back against the headboard, and he put his head on my shoulder, his hand on my thigh. He sighed but he didn't say anything else for a long time. I was trying to remember the last time I laid eyes on him. It was that first week of January when we went to see Angie in the hospital after she had the baby. I hated him so much then, as much as I had hated him all these years. But there was no hate in my heart for him at that moment, just sadness. Not sadness that he died but about the way he lived, with so much hate and disdain for everything and everyone that he didn't understand. And again, I felt relief. It was one less person in the world who hated me for who I am. Wherever he was, he was free from his hatred, and I was free of him. That thought brought me back to the dream of Vinnie, remembering that he told me I was already free. I wondered if that was what he was trying to tell me just now, that again, I was already free of him.

Jamel finally spoke, saying quietly, "I'm going to say it, because you need to get used to hearing it. People are going to say it to you everywhere you go for the next couple of days, maybe weeks. So you want to practice how you are going to respond. You're ready?"

I nodded. I knew what he was going to say, and he was right. *Because while others might be sorry, I am not.*

Jamel leaned up and looked me in the eyes. "Connor, I'm sorry for your loss," he said.

I stared at him. "Fuck." I sighed.

He nodded. "A simple, 'Thank you' would suffice, just so you know. You don't have to mean it. But it ends the conversation if you want it to."

"Fuck," I expressed again. "This funeral is going to be awful. All these people who either have no idea who he was and thought he was the best person ever, or people who knew exactly who he was and agreed with him. Either way, it's back in the closet for me, pretending like we have this perfect family and I'm their perfect son. I don't want to do this shit, Jamel."

"I know," he said, touching my thigh. "I'm right here for you to help you through it. And if you need me to go to the funeral, I will."

"I need you!" I practically yelled at him. "I don't give a shit what they say. You're my family. I need you."

He squeezed my thigh. "I know, Connor. I just meant that because of the history between him and I, the fight, the court hearing, it might seem inappropriate. It's not because of our relationship I considered not going to the funeral. But you're right. We're going, together."

I nodded. He put his head down on my thigh and stretched his arm across my lap. I unlaced his durag and messed up his hair, as I rubbed his head over and over again, but he didn't mind. He let it grow just a half inch off his head since the summer, and I liked his soft curls.

We sat in silence and then after a long while, he asked me, "Do you want to make love?"

I shook my head. "No. I just want to hold you like this."

"Okay, baby," he said softly.

We stayed like this, me sitting up in the bed with his head in my lap in silence, running my hands through his hair monotonously until the sun came up.

I drove over to my mother's house and parked in front of the garage. They never changed the locks, and I still had the key. I just wanted to see it, so I went to my old apartment first. It was frozen in time, exactly the way I left it back in 2010 when I moved out. My father beat me for the last time right here in this living room, just two days before I made my great escape. The furniture was still there, minus my bedroom set. The kitchen was completely bare. I sat down on the couch, and a layer of dust rose up. I leaned back and closed my eyes with memories. I made love to Afia on this couch. I made love to Jamel on this couch, too.

After a few minutes, I made my way back down the stairs and to the main house. The door was unlocked. I rang the bell anyway before I stepped inside, as was our custom. My mother was standing in front of the kitchen sink, holding onto the edge, staring out into the backyard. She turned her head to stare at me as I walked in. I expected her to be red-faced and have bloodshot eyes from crying all night, but she was eerily calm.

I stood next to her. She didn't move to give me a hug, but I didn't expect her to. I placed my hand on top of hers and said, "I'm sorry, Mom."

She nodded, then turned back to the window. "I know you hated him," she said softly.

I didn't respond to that. Instead, I asked her, "What do you need, Mom? I'm here for you, whatever you need."

She flipped our hands so that hers was on top and squeezed my hand. She spoke without looking at me. "I need you to listen to me, Connor. I just need you to listen and not talk. Because I need to tell someone, and you're the one who knows how to keep secrets. And after this, I'll never utter these words again."

My mouth opened slightly, as she was scaring me with how she was talking. I had never heard her use this hauntingly low voice before. But I said softly back, "Okay. I'm listening."

She swallowed twice, then grabbed the dish towel off the sink and started wringing it, as she told me what happened to my father.

"He hit me yesterday morning. I was knitting and wasn't moving fast enough for him, so he struck me across the face. Since everyone moved out, he had been doing it more and more. Backhanding me across the face."

I fucking knew it. She kept telling me everything was fine, but it was never fine with Owen, that abusive fuck. He didn't feel like a man unless he was beating on someone. I felt a burning rage in my chest, but I stayed quiet and let her continue.

"I don't know what possessed me to fight back but I did. I balled up my fists and hit him right back." She balled up her fists with the dish towel still in her hands and had a look of defiance on her face.

"Well, he had the upper hand as usual, and he really hurt me. Then he climbed on top of me to hurt me more." I knew what that meant. *And now I'm really glad he's gone. Now I wish I had done the deed myself all those years ago.*

"I went about my day after that. We went to Mass, and then we came home and had lunch. He said he was going upstairs to take a nap, and I stayed downstairs to knit. Then I started dinner around three o'clock. A little after four o'clock, I heard a loud thump. I called out his name, and he didn't answer. So, I went to go check on him." She paused, then said, "He had fallen out of the bed. He said he couldn't move the left side of his body. His speech was slurring. I know the signs. Owen was having a stroke." She paused again.

By now, I figured out where this was going. My mother was first aid/CPR-certified and had been all of our lives. She knew all the signs of a stroke, heart attack, choking, dry drowning, even a brain aneurysm. She knew time was of the essence with those things.

My mom asked me not to talk, but I wanted to encourage her to get it out, so it wouldn't eat her up inside. I said to her softly, "It's okay, Mom. Tell me what happened next. It's just me here."

She stopped wringing her hands, looked me in the eyes, and said, in the calmest voice I have ever heard her speak in, "I pulled up a chair and I watched him die."

I nodded slowly, staring into the icy blue eyes that she gave to me, to all of us. She turned away from me and looked out the window again, this time lifting her head up high in pride. "I sat there, and I reminded him of all the things he had done, to give him a chance to repent before he meets God."

I almost laughed. Good thing she wasn't looking at my face or she would have seen me smirk. I let her tell me what she told him.

"I reminded him of the first time he beat my oldest boy with a belt buckle. Matthew was three years old and broke something off his desk. That cruel man took off his belt and instead of hitting him with the leather side, he used the metal side. He made my boy scream and bleed. And when I tried to stop him, he broke my arm."

At three!?? Wow. What an abusive fuck. But I didn't say anything, letting her continue.

"I reminded him of when he put my oldest boy's head in the bathwater and drowned him when he was seven years old because he caught him masturbating in the water. Matthew died for sixty full seconds, and I had to bring him back to life."

Holy shit! Matty must have remembered that! I had never felt sadder for her than right then, having to bring her own son back from the brink of death. That was probably why she started learning all kinds of life-saving measures. She couldn't stop him, but she could save us if anything happened. I let her keep talking.

"I reminded him of the time when he beat my second boy's bottom red, because he didn't like the way he danced with his sister."

I remembered that. I was about six, and Mary Kate was about two. We were dancing to something and shaking our hips together. I never understood what I did to upset him so much, but he came out of nowhere, pulled my pants down and held me over his knee as he spanked me with his bare hand until I couldn't sit down, screaming at me that dancing with her was incest. That was my earliest memory of his abuse. To this day, I don't dance with my sisters.

"I reminded him of when he slammed your head into the wall." I definitely remember that. I had broken something of his, and he hit me a few times, then grabbed my head and slammed it so hard against the wall that I passed out and woke up in the hospital with a concussion. They told the doctors I was running so fast that I ran into the wall headfirst. I was nine, and it was the first time I knew to lie for him. I told that story at the trial.

"I asked him where he got the straightjacket from. He just came home with it one day. I reminded him of every single time he put you in it and hit you, then isolated you." *Too many times to count.* I would stand in the corner and memorize songs in my head while my family had to ignore me. For hours.

"I reminded him of what he did to my oldest daughter, how he slammed her down and slapped her around, making her bleed. I reminded him that for the second time, he tried to kill my oldest son right in front of me, beating him until he almost died. Then he put his hands around my throat while he got on top of me and hurt me. He tried to kill me too that night." The night none of us will ever forget. So much so it came out at trial and, of course, Matty denied it.

"I reminded him of when he put his gun to my oldest son's head and told him he would kill him dead if he ever disgraced the McIntyre name." That was after he got Stephanie pregnant. I didn't see it, but MK did and told me. "He did the same to you, Connor, and I reminded him of that too."

I'll never forget that. It was after my seventeenth birthday party. I had invited everyone, including Jack and Afia. He didn't realize until that day that they were two of the closest people in my life, a gay guy and a Black girl. After the party, he told me to meet him in his den, and I refused. I didn't know what I had done to deserve a beatdown on my own birthday, but there was no way I was going willingly. So, he went downstairs, came back with his Smith and Wesson and put it against my head. My mother and Matty were the only ones there; I don't remember where my sisters were. He told my mother that if she moved a muscle, he would shoot me in the head right in front of her.

He made me stand up and open wide. He put the barrel in my mouth and said to me that I was to never bring home any faggots, niggers, spics, kikes, chinks, liberals, or do anything that would embarrass or disgrace the family name, or he would blow my fucking brains out. Then he said, "On second thought, you're a worthless piece of shit, and I just wasted my breath on you. So, I'll just put you out of your misery now." Then he pulled the trigger. He didn't pull the trigger when he did it to Matty, but he pulled the trigger on me. Owen always kept his guns loaded, so I thought he had done it. The click alone made me fall backward to the floor, and my mother screamed. She thought he had done it too. I was seventeen on the seventeenth, and it was that day I decided it was my lucky number. And it was after that I made the decision to go into the military. I needed to learn how to kill him before he killed me.

"I reminded him of every single time he hurt me in that way he didn't need to. I was his wife. He never needed to force himself on me. I knew my duty. I reminded him of every single time he hurt all of us when he didn't need to. We were his family. I sat for an hour and reminded him of these things. Then I went downstairs and finished making dinner."

She left him to die. Holy fucking shit.

"I made his favorite meal and set the table, then at five minutes to six, I called him down for dinner. He didn't answer so I went to go check on him like a good wife. When I saw him lying on the floor, I screamed so the neighbors would hear me and called the police. They couldn't resuscitate him, so they took him to the hospital. They told me he had a stroke, and that it had been too long, and they couldn't save him, that he was most likely brain dead. They asked what I wanted to do."

She turned and looked me in the eyes again. "I waited another two hours before I called Matthew."

Ho. Lee. Shit. She wanted to make sure he was good and gone first.

"I told them not to call you. Only Mary Kate thought it was right to do so. But I knew you wouldn't care to come down. You just wanted to know when the deed was done."

I nodded slowly again. She turned away and said, "I killed him."

"No," I told her right away. "A stroke killed him. You just didn't help him because he didn't deserve to be helped."

"Maybe if he didn't hurt me that morning, I would have."

She pulled down the shoulder area of her top and showed me the black-and-purple bruise he left on the top part of her arm and the bite mark he left on her shoulder. It was still red, bleeding, and oozing puss. My mouth dropped. She quietly slipped the shirt back onto her shoulder, but I came behind her and lifted it up, and she did not resist. Her entire back was black and blue. I sighed.

I turned her around so she could face me and said, "You didn't put the dog down. God did. And you have nothing to feel guilty or bad about. Promise me you will never feel guilty about this." She didn't answer, just looked out the window. "I should have killed him eight years ago, Mom. I should have killed him, for you."

She turned to me, and we stood face to face. *My mother. The strongest woman I've ever known.* She moved into my chest and wrapped her arms around me, and I did the same. She wasn't crying, and neither was I.

The doorbell rang. We heard the door open and close, and I heard his voice. "Hey Mom, where are you? I worked it all out. McGillicuddy's got him now and the funeral is Sat—" He stopped short when he saw me.

I let my mother go and looked at him. "Hi, Matt."

He glared at me, then turned to my mother and said, "What the fuck is he doing here?"

She sighed. "Matthew, don't start."

"No, fuck that," he said nastily. "He didn't think it was important enough to say goodbye, then he doesn't need to be here either. He's not a part of this family anymore."

I said dismissively, "Yeah okay, whatever."

"No, fuck that!" he said louder. "In fact, get the fuck out of my house."

I looked at him like he was crazy. "*Your* house?"

"Yeah, cocksucker. Dad put the house in my name when he redid his will. He wanted to make sure you didn't receive a fucking thing from him. The house and the dealership are mine. His money goes to his girls. Mom gets his pension. You don't get shit."

I shook my head and chuckled. "I wouldn't take shit from him, and he knows it."

"Good, now get the fuck out of his house then. You don't belong here anymore. Go back to your butt-fucking family."

"Matthew!" my mother scolded him.

"No, you know what? It's all good, Matty. I'll get out of your house," I said casually.

My mother grabbed my arm. "Connor, no! I want you here."

I gave my mother a hug again. "I'll see you Saturday at St. Cecilia's. My sisters will give me the details."

As I walked out, Matty yelled after me, "Don't bother coming! He wouldn't want you there anyway. You were a fucking embarrassment to him."

"Fuck off, Matty. You're a fucking embarrassment to me. And to your son," I said right before the door closed.

I left there and went to work. As I was closing up business at the end of my day, Afia opened the leasing door, brightening my whole world. "Are you okay?" she asked with a hug. I didn't even ask how she knew, but I was glad she did.

"I'm fine, Lovie. I just want this week to be over so I can go back to my normal life," I told her.

"How are your mom and your sisters? I'm going to stop by there after I leave you here," she said, as she sat in the chair.

I thought of my mother. My strong, amazing mother. "She's holding up as best as can be expected. It's hitting MK pretty hard. I haven't spoken to Angie. They're staying there with Mom until the funeral. Fair warning if you go over there: Matty was there when I left, as his usual asshole self."

She shook her head. "I'm going over anyway, just to pay my respects."

"We'll do that at the funeral. No reason to go over there now."

Afia paused, then said, "Connor, I'm not going."

I grimaced at her. "What the fuck are you talking about? Of course you're going."

She shook her head again. "I'm not. Connor, your father hated me. I'm not going to his funeral."

"You're not going for him. You're going for me. To be there for me."

"No, you have Jamel for that," she said. "He'll be by your side, holding your hand. He's your person now."

"Afia, what the fuck!?" I yelled at her.

"Don't yell at me, Connor!" she yelled at me.

"How could you do this to me!?" I yelled back.

"Do what? Put myself back into an uncomfortable position like I've done for years? Pretend that he was a good man with a good heart and I'm one of the many people that will sorely miss him? Why the fuck would you even ask me to!?"

"Because *you're* my fucking person!" I yelled again. "You've always been there for me!"

"And I always will! But I know what your father really thought of me." She spat the next words at me. "Nigger bitch. Monkey bitch. Bed wench. Colored whore. I'm not going anywhere near his funeral unless you want me to spit on his fucking corpse!"

I never told her any of that. "Who told you that?" I asked her quietly.

She scoffed. "Connor." She looked away and confessed. "After we spent your whole leave together after prom and you went back to base, your father came to my father at the pharmacy. I was standing right there when he told my father that under no circumstances were we to be together and he gave him all the reasons why. He called me all those names and said it calmly and factually. My colored ass would never be good enough for his pure white son. He told my dad that if you ever got me pregnant, he would kill me and our nigger babies. My father had to pull the shotgun from behind the counter and tell him that if he ever put a hand on me or step foot in his pharmacy again, he would put a hole in his chest. That's where they left it."

I had to pick my jaw off the floor. "How the fuck could you keep that from me all this time?"

She shook her head again and gave me a look. "It wasn't anything you didn't already know. If he came to my father and threatened to kill our babies, then I know he threatened you over me."

I looked away and admitted, "More than once."

"I had to tell my father that you were gay and that we weren't together. That's the only reason he never held it against you."

I turned back to her. "But you let me drag you to Sunday dinners for five years and never told me what he said to you and your father? I would have never brought you into that house."

"You needed me. What was I supposed to do?"

"Tell me, Afia!" I started yelling again. "Tell me so I could have…"

I honestly don't know what I would have done. But I certainly wouldn't have asked her to come to dinner with me.

"You were afraid of him, Connor! I knew that you would never let anything happen to me, but you couldn't do anything, not really. Not while he still had his thumb on you." Afia sighed. "I told Jamel that night when he found out about him beating on you. And he told me that he would kill him if your father ever touched you again, and then extended that same promise to me."

I was stunned into silence. *Jamel knew and never told me either.*

"I'm not going to his funeral," she said. "No fucking way. I will be here when it's all over. But you cannot ask me to go. You can't. Let Jamel do this for you. I need to sit this one out."

Tears sprouted from her eyes, and she was shaking in anger. I had never seen her like that before.

I walked over to her and kissed her forehead. "Okay, Lovie. Okay."

CHAPTER 8

FEELINGS

Connor

I went to work every day that week. Nate stopped by to say hi on Tuesday. He did that from time to time. Jack was right, it seemed; he just wanted a friend. I'm not sure if that's what I was to him, but he didn't bother me anymore, and I didn't get stalker vibes from him. Attraction toward me, yes, but not in a, "I want to jump your bones" kinda way, more like admiration. He liked to pick my brain on random issues more than anyone else. I welcomed the distraction as he talked about his ex-wife and her getting engaged literally days after the divorce was finalized. But he got joint custody of his girls, and he hadn't had a drink in ten months, so he was okay. And I was happy to have a hand in that.

Jack and Ethan came by the house with their children on Tuesday evening and had dinner with us.

Neither gave their condolences for my loss, and I appreciated that from them.

"Mary Kate said the funeral is Saturday at 10 a.m.," I told them. "Are you going?"

Ethan scoffed and looked at Jack. Jack gave him a look first, then turned to me. "I'm going with my dad. Even though they weren't friends, Owen was a dedicated member of the small business council, so he feels it's only right to be there. Brayden and his dad are going too, for the same reason. Ethan feels no such obligation, despite also being on the council."

"No the fuck I don't," Ethan said definitively.

Jack gave him a look again. Then said, "I'm going for you, to make sure you're okay. I want to be there for you."

"That's because you're a good best friend," I told him, a lump forming in my throat, thinking of Lovie. She must have told him that she wasn't going.

"And I'm going for Freddie," said EJ. "I want to be there for my best friend too. And you too, Uncle Connor!" He said that last part as an afterthought, which made me smile at him.

"I will be home, praying for you. And I'll have an ice-cold 'Rona beer waiting for you when it's all over," Ethan said. "Because you'll have earned it." I smiled at him too.

❤

On Wednesday, Angie, Chad, and the kids showed up at my house. "Can we stay here?" she pleaded. "Matty is driving me crazy right now, barking orders and shit.

You know the expression, 'Who died and made you the boss'? Well, I think he's taking that shit literally." They made themselves comfortable and again, it was nice having the distraction.

Then the unthinkable happened on Thursday. Jamel woke me up around 5 a.m. "Connor. Wake up."

"Hmmm…"

"Open your eyes." I did. He hesitated, then said. "It's Diesel. He's gone."

I didn't speak for a moment, letting him continue. "I went downstairs to fill their bowls, and neither came up. I found Maje in the media room, staring out the backdoor. When I opened it, she ran out to him. Ang or Chad must have let him out sometime last night, and he never came back to be let in. It wasn't the cold though; I think he knew it was his time. He must have just laid there until his heart gave out."

I sat up slowly, my eyes adjusting to the darkness in the room. "I want to see him."

I got out of the bed, and Jamel followed me downstairs to the backyard, where my dog lay in the middle of the grass, dead. Maje was bouncing around him nervously, but when I sat down with him, she laid down next to me. I put Diesel's head in my lap and petted his cold skull, and I told him softly what a great dog he was, thanking him for always knowing when someone just needed a cuddle or extra attention, saying goodbye. Jamel came and knelt in the grass with me. I looked up when he started sniffling, tears accidentally falling out of his eyes. Then he stood up quickly.

He went over to the shed to grab a shovel and started digging under the lemon tree. I watched him make a hole at least three feet deep, then grab the large biodegradable garbage bags we use for recycling, and I helped him wrap our 60-pound dog in it. We had no idea if what we were doing was legal or not, but neither of us cared. After he was all wrapped up, we carried him together and put him gently in the ground, then used our hands to fill the hole. Jamel stood up while I stayed on the ground and looked at the fresh pile of dirt, feeling numb. *This is the last fucking thing I needed.*

I stood up, and Jamel tried to pull me into a hug, but I moved away from him. "I'm going to work," I told him, as the first rays of sunlight began to rise.

I was at my desk when Nate came by again. He never came by twice in the same week.

"Hey, Corporal McIntyre. Was your father Retired Army Staff Sergeant Owen McIntyre?" he asked.

"Yes," I said without looking up.

"He … he just died?"

"Yes."

"Ah … you didn't say … I'm so sorry!" he said sincerely.

"Thank you." I looked up at him. "Was there something you wanted?"

He looked at me stunned. "You're taking this pretty well."

"We were estranged," I told Nate. "Do you need something?" I asked again.

"No, I just … I read it in the paper. Just wanted to give you my condolences."

I nodded. "Thank you," I said again.

He hesitated in the doorway, then said, "Do you want to talk about it?"

"Absolutely not."

Nate surprised me with a smile. He made his way to my desk and sat on the edge of it, closest to me. He said, "My father was a bastard. He drank, beat the shit out of us, slept with several women, got them pregnant, and left them. I have twelve brothers and sisters that I know of, and only three of them between him and my mother. He died at fifty-one in a car accident, drunk as shit and taking someone with him. I didn't cry at his funeral, and I won't cry about it now. Fuck him."

That got a laugh out of me. Then he leaned over and touched my shoulder. "Sometimes the best thing fucked up fathers could do is show us how not to be. Only when I drink do I become him, so I try to stay away from it altogether. But I did everything differently than he did: Got married, stayed faithful, started a family, never hit my girls. That's how we become better men, doing the opposite of what they did. So, whatever fucked up things he did or said, thank him for it. It made you the man you are today. And from where I'm standing, you're a pretty good man."

"Thanks." I looked up and smiled at him, and he smiled back.

We heard the knock on the door, and he let my shoulder go as we turned to it. Jamel walked in with a stoic expression on his face.

"Hey," he said flatly.

"Hey." I got up and came over to him. He didn't reach for me or touch me; that was my first clue. "What are you doing here?"

"I came to check on you."

"Oh. Sorry about this morning. I walked around town before I got to work. Just needed to clear my head. I'm fine," I assured him.

"Yeah, I see that." He nodded toward Nate.

"Oh." I turned back to introduce them. "Nate, this is Jamel, my husband. Jamel, Nate."

"Sergeant Jones, good to meet you. I heard a lot about you," Nate said in a friendly way.

"Yeah? You shouldn't because I don't know shit about you. Except your name. Nathaniel Proctor," said Jamel, with a little edge to his voice.

Nate nodded in understanding. "I'm sure I haven't made the best impression. I'm sorry about that," he said apologetically.

Jamel glared at him in the same way he would glare at my brother. That was my second clue. *Uh-oh.*

Nate sensed it too, the danger. "Well, uh … I'm going to get going." Nate turned to me. "Sorry again, for your loss." Then he stepped out of my office.

As soon as the door closed, Jamel narrowed his eyes at me. "Connor," he called my name annoyedly.

I put my chin on his shoulder and my arms around him. I had to calm my lion down. "He just stopped by to talk, that's all," I said soothingly.

Jamel didn't say anything at first. Then he wrapped his arms around me and lifted me off my feet, squeezing me tight and making me giggle. I ended up with my arms around his neck and said, "I know, baby. I love you too."

He put me down slowly and kissed my lips. Then he said to me, "He's going to make a move on you. Be ready." I chuckled. He didn't. "I'm not fucking around, Connor. He's going to do it. I have a feeling about this."

"Okay," I said seriously. "I don't see that happening. But if it happens, I will handle it." He narrowed his eyes at me again. "I'll handle it," I said again. He breathed all the air out of his nose. I asked him, "What is it about Nate that has you fired up all the time? Is it because of the call, because we hashed that out and I'm not mad about that anymore. Or is it something else? You don't trust me anymore?"

Jamel never acts like a jealous partner, but he is now, and I'm really hoping our little adventure in Aruba doesn't have things changing about us. It is what I feared.

"What is it about the sanitation guy that has you sitting on the porch every Wednesday morning?" he asked me. "Do you not trust me?"

I told him the truth. "Because I fucking hate that guy. It's not about me trusting you; it's Jon I don't trust. I know he wants to fuck you, and you're not going to change my mind about that." *Because fuck that guy, if he hasn't made a move yet, he will, I know it.* Jamel will shut him down, but still, it put a bad taste in my mouth that he was so close, especially when I wasn't around. So, I made it my business to be around.

He looked at me amusingly with his eyebrow raised, like he could read my thoughts. *Fuck, Jamel got me.* "Okay, fair point," I said and rolled my eyes.

He laughed. "Just be ready, Connor. That's all I'm saying."

Now he has me suspicious. I narrowed my eyes at him. "Did Jon make a pass at you?"

He laughed again. "I wouldn't tell you if he did."

I frowned. "Why?"

He gave me a look. "So you can sit out on the porch with your coffee *and* Magnum? Nah. You already got one attempted murder charge under your belt. A second one would be a pattern."

I laughed out loud and kissed him on his lips. "Shut up."

He held onto me and said, "Happy anniversary, baby."

Shit, it's the seventeenth! We had decided to have a quiet night at home to celebrate our eleventh and third-year anniversary, but with everything going on, it totally slipped my mind.

"I'm sorry, I forgot. I feel like a terrible husband. Happy anniversary, baby." I gave him another sweet kiss on the lips.

"So, here's the real reason I came by. You're off tomorrow. I already told Ethan," he said. "I'm taking you away for thirty-six hours, starting now. Your bag is already in the car. We'll be back in time for the funeral, but we're leaving the house to Angie and Chad."

God, I love him. He always knows what I need. And what I didn't need was to go back into that house and not have my dog greet me. I can't deal with that yet.

I nodded. "Sir, yes sir."

He smiled, nuzzled his nose with mine and kissed the tip of my nose.

❤

We went to Aquidneck Island, reminisced about the first time we came there, and laughed about our almost sex. We sat on the beach and watched the sun set, reminiscing about our road trip to Florida and agreed to go back to Carolina Beach at some point. We went back to the hotel room and I made love to him, then we laid in bed sideways and held each other, talking softly, bringing up memories of the last decade plus one year that we'd been together.

We ended up talking about Aruba, dancing around what we both really wanted to talk about, until he brought it up, saying, "I loved seeing how free you were. Seeing a whole different side of you in bed. The ferocious side, the insatiable side. The BDSM side of you."

I chuckled. "I wouldn't go that far but … I've been known to restrain people a time or two. You gonna let me tie you up?" I winked.

"I've been waiting for you to ask me all year," he said, pinching my nipple and making me laugh. "But I figured you only save that wild side of yourself for when there is someone between us." He raised an eyebrow at me.

I looked into his silvers and said exactly what was on my mind. "I want to do it again," I told him. "Not because I want to fuck someone else, but I want us to fuck someone together. So, let's do it again."

He nodded slowly with a smile. "Okay."

"But I don't want to pay for it. So maybe let's find someone on Tinder willing to do it."

"Not someone we know and trust?"

I shrugged. "If we do, it has to be someone from your circle because we're too close to mine. Any more gay Army friends?"

Jamel laughed out loud. "So not Jack or Ethan?"

"Fuck no!" I said seriously, making him laugh again. "We got closer this summer than ever before, becoming Covid families and shit. Their kids are like our kids so, no." I shook my head vigorously.

"Covid families," he chuckled. "I like it. Okay. Someone from my circle. Let me think about it, who would be open enough to do it."

"Like Dante." I smiled without looking at him.

I have no idea why I just said that. Okay, I kinda do.

His eyes went wide, and his face turned up into a wide smile. "Dante? *Really?*"

I shrugged again. "I'm just saying. He's hot. And we don't see him enough for it to be awkward. And I know you don't see him like a brother like you do Ethan now. And you've already done it once, so..." I shrugged again.

"Holy shit Connor, you've thought about this," Jamel said, amused.

"Nooooooo ... It might have crossed my mind the first time we met way back when, but it hasn't since then. I mean ... not seriously crossed my mind..." He nodded sarcastically, then started laughing again. I groaned. "Okay, fuck it, forget I said anything."

"Oh hell no, I'm not forgetting shit. Cat's already out of the bag. I'm going to call him. And he's going to do it. Before you and me got together, he had been itching for a reason to get at me again since we did it all those years ago, and I've always shut him down. And he told me that day on the boat when you met him if I didn't scoop you up, he would." He winked at me. "He would definitely be interested in this. So, if you're serious …yay or nay?"

I paused. "Let me think about it." Because suddenly, just like before, it got very real.

"Okay," he said.

We continued to stare at each other, then I rolled him over, put my head on his heart, and fell asleep that way.

We spent Friday mostly in silence. We ate our meals in silence, we walked on the beach in silence, we took a drive around the whole island, in silence. I spent every moment in the moment with him, nothing and no one else mattered. We ended up on the beach watching the sun set again, him holding me closely to his chest. I knew the wake was happening that night, and the funeral was tomorrow morning, but I didn't want to think about any of it. I just wanted this time to breathe, and I didn't even know how much I needed it until now.

We didn't have sex that night. We got into bed and lay close, heads on one pillow, legs combined. Being close, being one person again. I broke the silence.

"I love you," I said softly.

"And I love you," Jamel said softly back to me.

"When was the first time you told me that you loved me?" I asked. "Before you actually said the words out loud to me?"

He answered, "That last night of our trip that we spent at Carolina Beach. The night you asked me if I was going back into the Army, then asked me not to leave you, and I told you I was never leaving you. It was the second time you asked me not to leave you, but this time you were sober." I chuckled softly. "You fell asleep before me. I already knew I was in love with you. I listened to the sound of you breathing, and I leaned over and whispered it in your ear. I thought you heard me because you sighed."

"Maybe my heart did," I said. "I did hear you one time though, the night of Jack and Ethan's wedding. I heard you say it, but I thought I was dreaming it."

Jamel smiled at me. "When did you tell me the first time?"

"Our first day in Florida. I woke up curled right next to you and you were sleeping, and I knew right then and there I wanted to wake up with you like that every day of my life. I kissed your skin, and I told you that I loved you. You didn't hear me."

"Wow. That trip to Florida changed everything for us, didn't it?"

"I guess it did."

He smiled. "So, you said it first."

I laughed. "But you *felt* it first."

"But you said it out loud; you made it real first," he said jokingly.

I laughed but then I said, "So what if I did? What if it was love at first sight for me?"

Jamel leaned in for a kiss and said, "Then it was always meant to be."

I crawled on top of him and let him hold me. I said a quick prayer, thanking God for bringing him to me when I needed him the most. I went to sleep feeling grateful and thankful for a partner that was always in tune with me. My perfect match.

I woke up before him. A feeling of dread washed over me, and I couldn't shake it. I felt paralyzed in bed for a long time and had to practice all the mindfulness and meditation techniques that I share with others when they feel a panic attack coming on. When I was finally able to get up, I went into the hotel shower, put the water on boiling hot, and stood underneath it, but I couldn't stop shivering.

Jamel came into the bathroom. "Connor, are you okay?"

I couldn't respond; my teeth were chattering. He opened the shower door, took one look at me, stepped in with his underwear still on, and pulled me into his arms. I couldn't even hug him back; I still had my hands clasped in front of me. He held me tighter as I put my head on his shoulder. I could hear him say softly, "I got you baby. I got you."

We stayed that way under the showerhead for a long time, long after I stopped shaking and melted in his arms. He said, "We don't have to go. We can stay here. Just tell me what you need me to do."

"I gotta go," I said to his shoulder.

"Okay. Do you want to make love first?" he asked. "And one drink. Just one shot of tequila, not twenty."

I smiled. *He knows me so well. But I can't. No more using sex and alcohol to avoid my feelings.*

"No. Whatever happens today, I need to feel all of it."

CHAPTER 9

MAY GOD HAVE MERCY
ON HIS SOUL

Jamel

Eleven years we've been together, and I have never been inside his home church. I know he missed it though, a lot. Being Catholic was not just his faith; it was part of his identity. He identified himself not just as Irish, but Irish Catholic. He carried a pendant of St. Christopher in his wallet for protection. He did the Eucharist and confession weekly at our church, and talked to Father O'Donnell, the priest from St. Cecilia's, like an old friend. I was agnostic for a while and had never really been sold on one denomination or another, which was why it was easy for me to convert to Catholicism and join Connor's church. Like most things in my life, I took the good parts and left the rest, and religion was no different. But I knew that

St. Cecilia's was home to him, with so many childhood memories at the center of it.

If he wanted to still attend this church, if he had ever asked me, I would have gone with him, but he never did. For him, going there would mean being under the scrutiny of the Rockville community, which included how the conservative Owen McIntyre was managing his gay son. Since we didn't live in Rockville, it was not an issue for us at all. But for him, as much as he loved his home church and his priest, he loved his life with me and his freedom from the deception of his picture-perfect family even more.

But I had to admit, it was a beautiful church. High round ceilings, glass windows depicting the final days of Christ, cushioned benches, and the Eucharist front and center. And it had a homey feeling to it, which was nice. The church was packed, despite social distancing rules still being needed, and it seemed like all of Rockville was there. There were Army vets as well, lots of people that Owen kept in contact with over the years, and some from his local lodge. I wore my Army uniform out of respect for his service, if not for him. Connor did not wear his Marine uniform; instead, he opted for a navy blue suit. I was trying to remember when I had seen him wear it before, and it was to Jack and Ethan's wedding. I tried not to think about the mind-blowing sex we had while he wore it when he came to my house after the ceremony.

We held hands and walked in slowly. We saw that his family had taken up the first three rows. His mother, his brother, and sisters sat in the front row with his eighty-four-year-old paternal grandmother, a couple of aunts, and an uncle that I've never met. Mary Kate was holding CJ, or C. Four, as Connor called him. Right behind them were their spouses: Stephanie, Dennis, and Chad, with Evie on his lap, and some other people I couldn't make out. And behind them were the grandchildren: Madeline holding her son with his husband Ivan, Deann, and Freddie, along with some other cousins that I didn't know, some from Owen's side of the family and some from his mother's. One of them must have been Scotty, Connor's favorite cousin who was in the Army but encouraged Connor to join the Marine Corps. It dawned on me how little I knew of my own husband's extended family.

As we walked together, he stopped halfway down the aisle and turned to look at me. We stared at each other, and he didn't have to say a word because I knew: he didn't want to go up there. I just said to him, "Okay."

I looked around and saw Jack, EJ, Brayden, and both of their fathers, Henry and Brian, who were in a row with room. Right behind them were BJ and Sam, a woman that looked just like them with auburn hair who had to be their older sister Moira with her husband, a woman I assumed was their mother, and the senior Mr. Jennings I remembered from the court hearing. I pulled Connor with me toward them, and Jack immediately stood up. They hugged tightly, then Jack moved over so we could sit with them. BJ and Sam also stood up and gave us both hugs. Their father narrowed his eyes at us, especially since we were still holding hands, but Connor did not see it. Connor thought that I didn't notice these things, but I did. I just didn't give a fuck.

We sat down and continued to hold hands. As the place filled up, I saw Freddie get up and walk the ten rows back to us with a Black Lives Matter mask on. I smiled. *This kid is always disturbing the peace, and I love him for it.*

"Hi, Uncle Con, Uncle Mel. Grandma said for you to come up there," he said.

We both glanced down and saw Connor's mother and brother in a heated argument. I guess Katherine wanted it, but Matty didn't. Connor looked at Freddie and said politely, "No. I'm fine where I am, thanks."

"Okaaay," he said in a singsong way and walked back down.

We watched Freddie relay the message. His mother paused for a moment, then slowly got up. Matty grabbed her arm, but she yanked it from him. Katherine walked down the aisle in her black dress and black veil attached to her big black hat, looking like the widow she was. She held her head high, and all eyes were on her as she walked to our row. She stood there for a moment as she and Connor stared at each other. Then she held her hand out. He hesitated, but then he took it and got up. She did not say a word as she walked a couple of paces, then turned around and looked at me. She reached out with her free hand and held it open for me to take as well.

I shook my head slightly. "No thank you, ma'am," I said quietly.

"You're family, Jamel," she told me in a stern but motherly voice, loud enough for everyone around us to hear. "Let's go."

I don't think she has ever publicly acknowledged me as family before. Despite the circumstances, I couldn't help the warm spot that formed in my chest. "Yes, ma'am," I responded immediately. I stood up and took my mother-in-law's hand.

When I got to her side, she said to me, "Your mother is here."

My mouth opened in shock and so did Connor's. "Where?" I asked.

"Come with me," she said.

She held both of our hands and walked us down, all eyes now on the three of us. And sure enough, as we got close to the first couple of rows, my mama was sitting there, in the second row right next to Chad. I almost cried at the sight of her. We hadn't seen each other in person since Thanksgiving last year. Because of Covid-19, we didn't make any plans to visit but video chatted weekly. I knew that she knew about Owen's passing, but I had no idea she was coming.

"Mama," I called to her as she came out of the row, feeling like her little boy again.

She reached up to his neck and hugged Connor first. "Go sit with your mama. Katie needs you," I heard her say in his ear when she kissed his cheek.

"I love you, Mama Denita," Connor responded, halfway bent over to her.

She lovingly touched his face with her silk-gloved hand that matched her dark blue dress, the dark blue wide-brimmed hat, and dark blue face mask. Then he moved to the front row and allowed his mother to seat him next to her on one side and Matty on the other, who was looking sullen.

My mother hugged me tightly. *I miss her hugs; I miss my mama.* "The Major is okay by himself?" I asked.

"Your daddy is fine. Now you come sit by me because you need me. I'll be your strength so you can be his."

"I do need you, Mama," I told her. "Thanks for coming."

Chad and Dennis made room, so I was sitting directly behind Connor and my mother was sitting behind Katherine. Freddie, who was behind me, leaned in and said, "I didn't know she was your mom. She's so fucking cool. She gave me strawberry candies." He pulled down his mask and stuck his red-streaked tongue at me.

I smiled and said, "She'll also put a bar of soap in your mouth if you don't watch your language, especially in church. Now sit back and shut up."

He laughed out loud, which made his mother glare at him and me, so he sat back again. My mother wrapped her little arm around my big one. Katherine held Connor's hand, as well as Matty's, as the funeral began.

The pallbearers brought in the casket, service men from his lodge. Prayers were made, songs were sung, and a scripture was read by a church member, the "Oh Death, where is your sting" one that is common for funerals. Another song, then Mary Kate got up and read John 14, another common one. Then Matty got up to do the eulogy.

"Family, friends, loved ones, on behalf of the McIntyre family, we thank you for coming to celebrate the life of Army Staff Sergeant Owen McIntyre. Our father, a beloved member of this community, a man of faith, integrity, honor, justice. A loving husband, father, and grandfather. A quiet man who held a lot of things inside, until there was a time to speak out and stand firm on the principles of God."

I knew how badly Connor wanted to roll his eyes by that point. Matty was sure to pile on the manure. And he did. Matty talked about all the wonderful things he learned from his father: how to fish and camp, how he taught them all how to shoot and hunt. How to be a husband and a father.

But then Matty said, "My father was not a perfect man. He made a lot of mistakes, even with his family. But everything he did, he did out of love for us. How much he fiercely loved and wanted to protect us from the evils of this world." He paused. "When I had my son, it was the happiest day of my life. I love my daughters, they know this. But once I had Freddie, my life became complete. My father came to the hospital the day after Freddie was born and held him in his arms. And for the first time in my life, I saw my father cry.

"He looked at me and said, 'You'll never know love and fear like you will when raising a son in this world. This world will try to take away his freedom, his rightful place, his God-given unalienable rights, try to erase what it means to be a man under the guise of equality for all. But we're not equal. The man is the head of the family, as Christ is the head of the church. And it's your job to teach him that he will not be equal; he will need to be above and to lead.' He told me that he tried to teach those things to his sons. And he admitted that at times, it came out harshly. Especially with me on one unspeakable night."

Whoa. I was stunned he brought it up, considering he denied it vehemently in court.

But Matty kept talking. "My father looked me in the eyes and said, 'I'm so sorry for what I did to you. To all of you. And all I want right now is for you to be the man that I never was.' You see, my father wasn't perfect, but he was honest, and he followed godly principles. You forgive and you ask for forgiveness. So right then and there I told him, 'I forgive you, Dad. We all forgive you. We know what was done was done out of love for us. So, Connor, Mary Kate, Angie, and I forgive you.'"

I kept my face straight, but I saw Connor's mouth open slightly. I know what Connor was thinking: Owen's declaration of contrition did not extend to his second son, who he continued to abuse for the next couple of years after Freddie was born, or to Mary Kate who he harmed that night too. Matty had no right to absolve their father for the rest of them.

Mary Kate leaned over to catch Connor's eye, also in disbelief, but he was glaring at his brother. She leaned back and shook her head annoyed. Angie, on the other hand, breathed out loud enough for us around her to hear, "Whaaaat an asshole." Chad squeezed her shoulder to calm her down.

Matty continued talking about his father's piety. "I've tried to raise my children with the same conviction that was taught to me. And like my father, I have made some mistakes. But also like my father, I will always be honest and true to myself, my faith, and my values. I will always stand on biblical principles, even when other members of my family go astray. And that is something that we can all learn from him."

That was an obvious dig at Connor, going astray by being gay. I imagined Connor in my head saying, "Fuck him for that," and it made me smile.

Finally, Matty ended it with, "I am honored and proud that this man was my father. And I will continue to carry the beliefs and values he has given to me. Thank you."

He walked over and hugged his mother, ignored Connor, who didn't make any moves to get up anyway, and hugged both his sisters. Matt reached behind and shook Chad and Dennis's hands, then had the nerve to look at me as if he was going to shake my hand too. I gave him an icy glare, wishing my mother wasn't right next to me so I could have given him the finger. He did a slight head nod and shook my mother's hand instead, then hugged his wife last before he sat down.

I could feel Connor's energy. He was tense and stressed. But he also kept his face unreadable as Father O'Donnell took to the podium for the last scripture reading and the Homily.

He opened his Bible and read Romans 14 in a loud and clear voice, "Accept him whose faith is weak, without passing judgment on disputable matters." He paused for dramatic effect.

"One man's faith allows him to eat everything, but another man, whose faith is weak, eats only vegetables. The man who eats everything must not look down on him who does not, and the man who does not eat everything must not condemn the man who does, for God has accepted him. Who are you to judge someone else's servant? To his own master he stands or falls. And he will stand, for the Lord is able to make him stand. One man considers one day more sacred than another; another man considers every day alike. Each one should be fully convinced in his own mind. He who regards one day as special, does so to the Lord. He who eats meat, eats to the Lord, for he gives thanks to God; and he who abstains, does so to the Lord and gives thanks to God. For none of us lives to himself alone and none of us dies to himself alone. If we live, we live to the Lord; and if we die, we die to the Lord. So, whether we live or die, we belong to the Lord. For this very reason, Christ died and returned to life so that he might be the Lord of both the dead and the living. You, then, why do you judge your brother? Or why do you look down on your brother? For we will all stand before God's judgment seat."

Father O'Donnell closed his Bible and said, "I had the pleasure of knowing Owen very well for over forty years. He will give his own account to God for the things he has done and not done and the judgments he has passed, as we all will. May God have mercy on his soul."

And then the priest stepped down from the podium to begin the communion part of the funeral Mass. I showed no expression on my face, but inside I was saying, *That's it!? Holy shit!*

"Well, that was … interesting," Chad said, next to Dennis. I couldn't help but smirk again, and I saw Connor did too. *Maybe we should be going to St. Cecilia's.*

After we took communion, Father O'Donnell blessed the casket with holy water and incense, and the pallbearers led the casket back out while we followed behind. Connor and I held hands again, trailing behind everyone else. When we got outside, we stood at the top of the steps and watched the congregation hug each other and mingle. He never let my hand go unless it was to hug someone who came to hug him, and then he grabbed my hand again.

Freddie came back to us with another message. "Grandma wants to know if you are riding with us in the limo to the cemetery. You too, Uncle Mel. Or are you gonna walk?"

I looked at Connor. "No," he said. "We're not going. But we'll be at the house for the reception."

"Okaaay," Freddie said, again in that singsong voice, as he walked away.

"You're okay?" I asked him. He gave me a look. I nodded. "Almost over. Then we go home, get drunk and … mourn."

I palmed his bottom, right on the church steps. He busted out laughing, and I pulled him in for a hug.

"That's a sound I haven't heard in a long time," a voice said behind him. We pulled apart, and Father O'Donnell was there. He had kind brown eyes like a loving grandfather, and a calming smile.

"Connor." He said his name as a greeting and held out his hands.

Connor left my arms and went into his priest's. Father O'Donnell rubbed his back and said, "He said, 'I do not think the whole world could have been as heavy on my shoulders as you were.' That is how I felt about you today. Our beloved St. Christopher was right."

I had no idea what that meant, but Connor looked up and smiled widely at him. "Thank you," he said softly.

"I'm glad you came. I didn't think you would, but I'm so glad you did." He patted his back and then looked up at me. "And this is the partner I have heard so much about."

Connor turned around and introduced us. "Yes. Father O'Donnell, meet Sergeant Jamel Jones. My husband."

He shook my hand and said, "It's great to meet you, son. I'm sorry we didn't get a chance to meet at the vigil last spring."

"It's good to meet you too, Father," I said. "Connor talks about you all the time; he misses your sermons. And that was a pretty great one in there. Thank you for it."

He smiled at me, then at Connor and winked. "I'm heading to the cemetery. Are you coming?" Connor shook his head no. "Okay," said the priest casually. "You've done enough. More than enough." He patted his back. "Don't be a stranger. Come visit me sometime, even for Mass. You've always been free to do so, but I suspect you'll feel like you can now."

"Thanks, Father," he said. The priest walked on.

We held hands and walked over to Connor's parents' house.

CHAPTER 10

FAMILY TIES

Jamel

I had only been in their family home once, many years ago when he was still in the closet, and I picked Connor up one day after Sunday dinner. I didn't need to come in, but more than anything, I wanted to look Owen in the eye and make sure he knew that I was still around in Connor's life, even if he thought we were just friends. But I always suspected he knew we were more than that.

There were a few people already there, including Angie and her family. Mary Kate and Dennis went with Matty and his family to the cemetery for the last rites and burial. Connor took me upstairs to his old bedroom and closed the door. He sighed deeply and laid on his full-size bed, staring at the ceiling. I laid down with him, both our feet hanging off the edge. I looked around at his wooden bedroom set and small

TV sitting on the wooden chest. He had a shelf of trophies and medals from his baseball days, and a closet that was still full of clothes and shoes; when he left, he didn't want to take anything with him.

We were quiet for a moment, then he said, "I used to lay here and watch *Queer As Folk* just to jack off to it."

A moment passed, then we both started laughing. "I wanted to be Brian Kinney," he said. "I think I was for a while."

"*OZ*," I told him. "That was the show I beat off to."

"I fucked a lot of girls in this room. A lot. I felt nothing for them. Except Winter. I liked Winter. She talks dirty like I do and made me laugh in bed. Which was probably not a reason to sleep with her, but it's why I kept doing it." He chuckled to himself.

"You fucked Jack in this room too," I said knowingly. "Right here on this mattress."

He laughed. "I did do that. More than once." Connor looked at me and smiled. "Want me to fuck you in this bed too, make it even?" He winked.

I laughed out loud, turned to my side, and pulled him close to me. "I love you, Connor. I love every single thing about you. I love how you make me laugh. I love the way you make me feel when I'm with you, even after all this time. I don't know where I would have been without you in my life, but it couldn't have been better than what I have now."

Connor turned to his side and looked at me lovingly. "You already know, Jamel. I fell in love with you, and my whole life changed. I grew up being with you. I still have some growing to do, I know. I know you feel like I'm emotionally immature and I snap out too quick." He paused.

I started laughing and said, "Go on! I'm not going to fucking disagree with you!"

He pushed my arm playfully. "Asshole," he muttered with a smile, making me laugh again. "What I'm saying is, I'm stronger, mentally and emotionally, because of you. I just needed a reason to grow up, and you gave it to me. And even if we never actually got together, I have a feeling just you being in my life would have motivated me. I never needed us to fall in love; I just needed you in my life. But I'm so glad every day that we did fall in love. That I didn't run from this, from you. I know you think Vinnie was the greatest love of my life, but he wasn't. You are."

"Well, I figured that when you asked me to marry you. You know, for healthcare purposes and all." I winked at him, and he smiled at me.

We kissed and held each other and laid there for a while, until Angie knocked on the door. "Hey, guys. Everyone is back. You're coming down, right?" Connor sighed.

"Get your game face on, Corporal. One hour, tops. You're ready?" I asked him.

He nodded. "Let's do it, baby," he said.

It all went to shit after that.

We mingled and stayed close to each other. Connor did not drink at all. He held my hand and proudly introduced me to everyone as his spouse. He introduced me as his husband to his paternal grandmother, who told me I was a "handsome colored man," and thanked me for my service. His aunts and uncle were loving and affectionate toward him and respectful to me. He played with his younger nieces and nephews, and we talked with his cousin Scotty, who was still in the Army, and other cousins who shared stories with me of a young, spirited, and reckless Connor whose mouth was always getting him into trouble. The positive response he received from his family members made him relax and bring his guard all the way down. It was actually going okay, so after an hour when I asked him if he wanted to go, he told me he was fine, and we stayed. It felt like we were actually building family ties with the McIntyres, which made him happy, so it made me happy.

Later, it had thinned out to where it was family and a few close friends like Sam and his dad, Jack, his dad and EJ, and Brayden and his dad. Katherine said she wanted to lie down, and my mama went upstairs with her.

I had noticed the whole time that Matty was drinking a lot. He would glare at Connor from time to time, and it seemed like he didn't appreciate Connor being accepted by his family. I don't know what made him come over and approach him; he's more of a mumbler and instigator, but every once in a while, he gets to smelling himself. And he did so this time, aggressively.

Matty walked over to us and said loudly, "Time's up, punk. Get the fuck out of his house."

Connor turned to look at him. "Why don't you go cool off somewhere, Matt?" he said, as he too could see Matty was drunk.

Matty shoved his shoulder. "I said get the fuck out!" he yelled. "Nobody fucking wants you here! They're all just being nice because no one wants to say to your face what they are all thinking."

"And what are they thinking, Matty?" Connor said calmly. I was shocked he didn't react to his brother shoving him.

"That you're … disgusting. That you're a sexually immoral cretin that should be eradicated from the face of the earth. That you're fucked up in the head and in the dick. Sticking it in this charcoal-looking mother-fucker." He spat that last part at me.

I was ready to yank his brother up, but Connor patted my chest before I made a move. That was his way of telling me, "I got this."

He turned to face his brother. "Matty, maybe you need to be less concerned about where I'm sticking my dick and more concerned with your sorry-ass life. Because from what I'm seeing, you're well on your way to becoming a bitter old man." I knew he wanted to say, "Just like your father" but he left that part out. He smiled at him instead.

Matty swung at him, and Connor leaned his entire torso back, so it completely missed him, then he pushed Matty hard.

"The fuck are you doing?" he said angrily. "You wanna fight me, Matty?"

"Get the fuck out of his house!" he yelled at him. "You don't deserve to be here! You think he'd want you here? He hated you!"

Mary Kate scolded him, "Matty!"

"I'm just telling the truth." He shrugged. "He fucking hated that Connor became a faggot! He's always hated him!"

"That's enough!" I said loudly. But Connor patted my chest again and stood in front of me, probably to keep me from knocking the shit out of his brother.

"You're right; he hated me, and I hated him. What's your point?" he said, again calmly.

Matty scoffed. "He always knew, you know. He always knew you were going to be fucking fruitcake. That's why he beat the shit out of you so much."

Connor shook his head and rolled his eyes. "Yeah, okay Matty. Fuck off with—"

He cut him off. "He told me when you were ten!"

That stunned Connor into disbelief. "What!? What the fuck are you talking about, you asshole!?"

Matty started laughing like shit was funny. "He told me ... that you were going to be a faggot. When you were ten years old," he said again, all smug and chuckling.

It was quiet, and I knew everyone in the room was listening. "Shut the fuck up, Matty," I said threateningly. "Stop talking, or I swear to God—"

"Let him talk," Connor said sternly to me over his shoulder. "Let. Him. Talk."

This is bad. This is going to get very, very bad. Every nerve in my body told me that. I should have gotten him out of there right then and there, but I was following Connor's lead, considering it was his family.

Matty said, "You were ten, playing right here in this living room with Mary Kate and Angie. You were sitting there in some too small shorts with your legs crossed, just enjoying time with the girls. Dad and I were watching baseball, and you were on the floor playing with beads and shit like a little bitch. I laughed, pointed at you, and said 'Hey Dad, I think you have three girls instead of two.' And he looked at me all serious and said, 'One day your brother is going to come home with an earring in his ear and a boy on his arm, switching his ass around. I can try to stop it, but if you catch it before I do, shoot him right between the fucking eyes.'" Then Matty laughed again.

I kept my face straight, but I glanced over at Connor, whose face was also unreadable. I know that shit hurt to hear but he made no indication of it. Instead, he said softly, "Is that right?"

"Yeah, that's right," Matty said nastily. "That's why he was always beating on you. He was disciplining me but you, he was trying to beat that homo shit right out of you. That's why he put a gun to your head and pulled the trigger, because of Jack. You know he had a bullet in there, right? Just one, trying to see if it was your turn to die. That's why he was still kicking the shit out of you until you were twenty-six. That's why he put you in chokeholds regularly, broke your ribs like once a fucking year. Hanging around faggots and shit. That's why he left the whole thing with Afia alone. I mean, she's still a nigger bitch but at least she had a fucking pussy!"

"Matty!" Mary Kate yelled at him again. "What the fuck!"

"You fucking two-faced bastard!" Angie started screaming at him.

She was holding the baby but practically threw poor C. Four in Chad's arms and started running toward Matty, with her fists balled up. Dennis moved fast and scooped her up, as her legs and arms started flying, and carried her to the other side of the room. She continued to scream at him about how he's an asshole, dickhead, and all the other curse words she could think of.

Matty laughed at her, threw his hands up, and said, "Hey, don't shoot the messenger. He called though." He laughed again. "Look at this faggot now!"

"What do yer think yer doing, Matty?" Ben Jennings Sr. spoke in a heavy Irish accent. "Yer think this is what yer father would have wanted? You telling all his business out here, in fronta everyone? Owen was a private man. How he felt about his sons was between him and his sons."

He scoffed. "No point in hiding it now. The man's dead. And knowing his son was out there sucking dick and fucking dirty-ass niggers sent him to an early grave."

I was over him dropping the word nigger around. I pushed Connor out of my way, but he stepped in front of me again and said quietly, "No."

"You think you're honoring him with this?" Jack's father, Henry Frazier, said angrily. "You're not. You're just disrespecting everyone in this room with your antics." Mr. Jennings and Mr. Frazier started arguing with Matty, as Connor and I argued quietly.

"Connor—" I said quietly back but he cut me off.

"No. I'll handle it. Stand down," he said back quietly.

"Fuck!" I mumbled.

"Stand down," he said again, through his teeth.

Matty noticed our murmuring. "What, you're going to sic your nigger bodyguard on me? Well come at me, *bro*!" he said sarcastically. "I'm not scared of a faggot like you either!"

"Ain't gonna be any more 'faggots' coming out of your mouth, Matty," Jack said, moving forward. I didn't even know he was in the room. He already had his hands balled up. "You already got fucked up by this one, don't get fucked up by two right now."

Connor moved quickly and jumped in front of Jack's path. "No. I got it," he said, eerily calm, like he was picking up a dinner check. "Sit this one out." He patted Jack's chest like he did mine.

They stared at each other as Matty started talking again. "What the fuck? You know what? It's too many of y'all in here. So all the niggers and faggots, get the *fuck* out of *my* house. Noooooooooow!!!" he screamed, face turning purple with anger.

Connor turned his head and locked eyes with me. They were hooded and hollow. Dangerous. Maybe I should have grabbed his hand and pulled him from the house, but I was beyond pissed too. So, I didn't stop him.

He turned around and faced his brother, walking slowly closer. "Say it again, Matty. Give me a reason. Just one," he said quietly and calmly.

Matty scoffed again. "Fuck you, you fucking pussy ass faggot. Take you and your nigger bi—"

Connor threw a quick right jab and hit Matty squarely in the mouth. Matty stumbled backward, grabbing his chin, and I smirked. So did Jack.

He flexed his knuckles and said quietly, "Say it again, Matty."

"Fuck you!" he yelled at him, with his hands still covering his face, bottom lip bleeding.

Connor nodded and turned around. He came up to me and said, "Let's go."

He reached for my hand, and we turned around together. But Matty just had to open up his big-ass mouth again.

"Yeah, get the fuck out and take your nigger bitch with you."

Connor stopped walking, and this time he didn't look at me at all. He let my hand go, turned, and walked back the way we had already come, while taking off his suit jacket.

Matty started bouncing around. "Yeah, let's go, motherfucker. Fucking faggot. Let's see if the Marines really did toughen you up. Pussy-ass, bitch-ass, dirty dick-ass motherfucker!"

Connor handed his jacket to Jack and rolled up his sleeves, then loosened his tie but just a bit. He turned around, and Matty was still bouncing around like he was Muhammad Ali, getting ready for a boxing match and looking stupid. Connor, however, was poised and calm.

I had actually never seen Connor in a fight. I have heard him threaten to kick someone's ass, including my own, more times than I can count, but to actually witness it was a thing of beauty, even though it was with his unskilled brother who obviously never won a fight in his life. Connor's training had done him well.

Matty had both hands up; Connor did not. He swung on Connor first, and Connor dipped back again, as smooth as Neo in *The Matrix*, and pushed him, then scoffed. Matty turned around and swung again, a wild one, and Connor side-stepped, turned around, and elbowed him right in the space where his neck and his shoulder met. Matty howled.

"Don't hurt him, Connor!" Mary Kate whined.

"Shut the fuck up, Mary Kate!" Angie yelled at her. "Kick his fucking ass, Connor!" she growled, Dennis still holding onto her.

If Connor heard his sisters, he made no acknowledgment of it; as Matty again tried to swing on him, Connor grabbed his arm and jabbed him in the nose with the palm of his hand. It immediately started bleeding. Matty howled again as he grabbed his face. He was really mad now, and he rushed at Connor's midsection, pushing him over the back of the couch where Jack was standing. Jack casually moved out of the way as they rolled off the front of the couch, tussling on the ground until Connor punched his back. He kicked Matty off him, and I heard his shoe connect with a leg bone. Matty cried a third time. Connor tried to stand up, but Matty grabbed his leg and bit him.

"Fuuuck!" Connor screamed.

He kicked again, this time in Matty's face, which made Matty howl again. Then he turned around and swung once, twice, three times directly to Matty's face. They both rolled over into kneeling positions, Connor getting there first, then started tussling again, grabbing at each other's arms. Then Connor headbutted him, hard, and Matty's head flew backward. I was beginning to enjoy this fight.

But then Connor moved quickly. He loosened his tie completely, wrapped it around Matty's neck twice, and pulled. And I knew in my heart that he would not let go.

"Fuck!" I yelled and ran over to him, getting on the floor with them and grabbing both his arms from behind him. "Let go, Connor," I said in his ear. "Let go."

I pulled but all of a sudden, he had superhuman strength. He leaned backward with me, taking Matty by the neck with him. We were almost laying down: me on my back, Connor still kneeling but my flexible husband leaned back too, his back on my chest, and Matty leaned over him. He wrapped both legs around him as his brother clawed at the thin piece of material around his throat. Jack joined me, pulling at Connor's arms on one side while Chad came out of nowhere and tried to pry his hands off the tie. The three of us tried our hardest to no avail, while I kept pleading with him to let go. But instead, Connor did the opposite. He reached his hands outward and wound the ends of the tie around both of his wrists and pulled Matty closer to him by his neck. People were screaming all around us.

I watched Matty lose oxygen, his eyes become bloodshot, his legs flailing around but less so the longer it went on. Connor had the coldest look on his face, almost smirking. My husband had gone elsewhere, to that place that sustained him back in Iraq, where he could take a life and not think twice about it. I started getting really scared that he was going to do it, that he was going to kill his brother in front of all these people.

The powerful phoenix in him had risen, dark and dangerous, and there was nothing I could do to stop him.

I tried again. "Connor please, baby, please let him go, please. Please don't do this," I said in his ear. "Let go baby, let go."

If Connor heard me, I don't know because the next thing that happened was that me, Connor, Jack, Chad all fell backward, and Matty fell over to the right of us. Angie was standing there with a pair of scissors; apparently, she snipped the end of the tie closer to Matty's neck. I looked up at her, and she had a look of disdain on her face for her eldest brother. Matty was gasping for air, coughing, and throwing up, his fingernails bloody. His neck had scratch marks and a bleeding line right across it where the fabric of the tie dug into his skin. It looked like Freddie's neck last spring, but ten times worse.

Connor was leaning against my chest backward, taking short, rapid breaths. I wrapped my arms around him and said gently, "At ease, Corporal."

I rubbed his chest and abs over and over again until he grabbed my hand and squeezed it, then started taking deep breaths to calm himself down.

Matty passed out. Madeline tried to revive him, calling "Daddy! Daddy!" over and over again, but he was unresponsive. "Call an ambulance!" She looked at us and screamed, "Get ooooouuuutt! Get the fuck out!

Get ooooouuutt!" Stephanie ran over too, her eyes wide in shock.

I tapped Connor, and he got up. He avoided my gaze, but he was completely composed. Jack, also composed, casually helped him put on his suit jacket, both of them acting like he didn't just try to kill his brother in front of about twenty people. I don't think I realized how alike they were until that moment.

Then I heard Matty's wife say nastily, "Just like he said, all faggots and niggers get the fuck out of our house! That includes all of you!"

The three of us looked at Stephanie, then Connor shook his head and reached for my hand. Jack was right behind us as I led him out the living room. Chad, who I've never seen angry ever, snarled at her. "God, you're a stupid, prejudiced bitch just like him!" He scoffed and walked toward Mary Kate, who was holding Evie in the corner so she wouldn't see what was happening.

As we were walking toward the door, EJ ran up to his father with Freddie on his tail. Connor did not acknowledge the boys at all.

"Pop!" he cried, wide-eyed. He looked afraid too.

Jack touched his shoulders. "I'm going with my friend because he needs me. Stay, and be here for yours." He looked beyond his son to Freddie, who also had a look of horror on his face. "You okay, Fred?"

"I…" He trailed off as Connor and I kept walking. He looked at his parents on the floor, then back at Connor. We locked eyes and he said to me, "I'm going with you."

Stephanie heard him and yelled, "No, you are not, get back here!"

He screamed at his mother, "Are you fucking crazy!? I'm not staying here with you! I'm going with my family!"

Freddie started walking behind me. I glanced at him and then put my arm around his shoulder. *I love this kid's conviction.* Jack and EJ followed us out.

As we walked through the front door, I heard Madeline say, "Where the hell do you think you're going?"

And I heard Deann answer her, "Y'all said gays included too, right? Well, I'M FUCKING GAY!"

A second later, Deann was right behind Jack and Ethan Junior. Freddie left me and went to his sister. "Holy shit, Dee. What the fuck was that?"

"I don't know," she said, as her voice shook. "What did I just do, Freddie?"

Freddie laughed and said, "Don't worry, Uncle Con and Uncle Mel have a lot of room in their basement."

I turned back and chuckled at Freddie, who smiled at me. Connor did not smile or even seem to know anyone was with him, except me, as he held my hand tightly, using me as his anchor. He stared blankly ahead as we walked down the street. He also failed to notice the trail of people behind him, starting with Jack, EJ, Freddie, and Deann. Then Angie and Mary Kate came running out of the house, with Chad holding C. Four again and Dennis holding Evie's hand, who was innocently holding on to the end of the tie that bound our little group together. Brayden and Sam were the next two people that came out, and I did not know they were still in the house until then. Both of their fathers stayed, as well as Jack's.

Angie yelled Connor's name repeatedly, but he did not respond. She had to run up to him and grab his other hand. He glanced at her but then turned his face ahead and kept walking. Mary Kate came to my left and grabbed my hand. And the four of us walked down the street holding hands together, with a trail of people behind us, destination unknown.

CHAPTER 11

QUEER ASS FOLKS

Connor

We ended up being steered toward Inn Love at the B&B, Jack and Ethan's place. I took off my suit jacket and white shirt, stupidly about to ask myself what happened to the tie I was wearing, leaving on a white tank top. I took off my shoes and socks, and I sat in the first chair I saw in the dining room, putting my feet up in another chair. Jamel took off his Army jacket, leaving on his black t-shirt, and sat next to me. He casually threw his arm behind my chair and gently massaged the nape of my neck with his fingertips. I felt myself slowly begin to melt, my anger receding little by little. I closed my eyes and focused on his touch, the coconut-scented oil he put on, and the internal sound of my heartbeat. I heard people move around me, Jamel talking to others, chuckling as someone made him laugh. Everything sounded far away, and the only thing left was my heartbeat and Jamel's scent and touch.

I almost killed my brother.

The revelation that my father knew that I was gay was like ice water to my veins. A chill went through me, as if his ghost was there, walking through my body, taunting me. *And there was his son, right in front of me, taunting me. Channeling his racist and homophobic father. Trying to embarrass me by spilling our family secrets and the reason I got the brunt of his abuse. Trying to shame me for who I am. Using words to try to hurt the love of my life.*

I was done. I was so fucking done. Done with Owen. Done with Matty. Done with everything and everyone that ever made me feel like I was wrong for the way I am and the way I love. It was going to end today.

I didn't set out to kill him. I was just going to knock some sense into him. But once I started hitting him, I knew where it was going to end. So, I didn't think; I just reacted on instinct and figured it would just look like a fight gone wrong when it was all said and done. If I thought about it, I wouldn't have been able to do it, but I wanted to do it. I wanted to kill him. I wrapped my tie around his neck the same way he did to my nephew because I wanted him to know what it felt like. He was going to die the same way he tried to kill his own son, the boy I loved like he was my own. It might sound horrible, but I loved watching the fear in his eyes when he knew he was going to die. The horror when he knew that it was happening, and that my face was the last face he was going to see on this earth. It literally made my dick hard.

Jamel's voice was the only voice I heard. I heard him telling me to let go, but I knew he would be the least upset if I accidentally snapped Matty's neck. I saw my husband's face every time he dropped the N word. That hurt him more than calling him a fag, because he was the only Black person in the room. I would have killed Matty for that alone. So, whether it was for me, or for Freddie, or for Jamel, or all of us, it needed to be done. Matthew Owen McIntyre was going to cease to exist, and I was going to be the one to do it. That thought gave me great joy. And then the tie snapped.

"Connor."

I opened my eyes, and Ethan was sitting directly in front of me. He slid me an unscrewed beer. "Corona. Because you earned it," he said. I sighed and took a sip.

Ethan slid one over to Jamel too. I looked over at my husband, and he was watching me. "You're back?" Mel asked.

I nodded. "Thank you."

He shrugged nonchalantly. Still cool as a cucumber. I knew I scared him though, but he'll never tell me.

Jack was sitting there too, across from Jamel. "Never a dull day in small-town Rockville, huh?" he said, as he leaned back and poured beer into his mouth, making Ethan laugh.

I looked around. There were a lot of people in the room. My friends. My family. "Where are the girls and Jamie?" I asked them.

"With Jack's mother," Ethan answered. "As soon as Jack called me, I brought them over there and opened up the doors here. Wanted to make sure you had a safe space to go."

"That's because you're a good best friend," Jamel said to him, mocking me, making me smile for the first time.

"Not better than me," Jack said smugly. "When was the last time you went to jail for your best friend, hmmm?"

I laughed as the door opened. Mina, Winter, and BJ came in, both the women baby-wearing their infants, five month old Benny and four month old Samson.

"Oh my God, Connor!" Mina said first and threw her arms around my neck. She grabbed my face and looked me in the eyes, searching. For what, I wasn't sure. Maybe she too wanted to make sure I was still me.

"I'm okay, Mina. I'm okay," I told her.

Winter knelt down and touched my face too. "I wish I could have been there to see you beat the skin off that asshole, once and for all," she snarled.

"Yeah, Sam said he would pay money to see it again," Mina said, as Sam came around and put his hands on his wife's shoulders. Brayden was right behind him. She patted my shoulder and said seriously, "Good job, Con."

I smiled at her. "Where's Lovie?"

"We don't know. I tried her cell like a million times," Winter said. "I left her a voicemail telling her what happened. She'll be here, don't worry."

I nodded, but for the first time in twenty years, I wasn't completely sure she would be there. I hadn't spoken to her since Monday, when she told me she wasn't coming to the funeral. It was the longest we had gone without speaking to each other.

BJ reached over the women to grab my hand. "You okay? For real?" I nodded. He nodded back. "Thanks for not killing him. You should have. I wouldn't have blamed you one bit if you did. But I'm glad you didn't." He sighed. "I'll be back. I'm going to pay my dickhead friend a visit," he said, shaking his head.

"Why are you still friends with him, BJ?" Jack asked. "I never understood that friendship y'all have. You're nothing like him." Jack said all the things I've wondered for years.

BJ sighed again and looked away, then turned back to us. "Matty is fucked up in the head for all the same reasons you hate him, because of Owen. Sam and I know what that's like, having a father with fucked-up views. We just never really bought into it because we had other people around that taught us differently. Like our aunt Lacey and our Black aunt Amina, and our cousin Chris, who is Black and gay. Everybody hates Matty, and you all have every right to. But I'm all he's got left. I can't turn my back on him." He shrugged. "But I'll say this, it's wearing thin, this friendship we got. Because my son isn't all the way white, you know." He looked at Winter, who smiled at him. Her mother's side of the family is from Brazil. "Anyway, I'll be back."

BJ walked out, and the rest of my friends pulled up chairs and sat with us. "Sam and Brayden told us what he said. Why did he say all those horrible things?" Winter asked. "He made your father sound like a monster."

"That's because he was a monster," I said quietly, as I looked down at my fingers. Jamel continued to stroke my neck, giving me strength. "It's all true. The beatings, chokeholds, the broken ribs. All until I moved out right before I turned twenty-six. Matty was telling the truth. That's how I knew he wasn't lying about my father either. My father suspected I was gay all this time. As soon as Matty started talking, I knew he was telling the truth."

I don't remember that day exactly, but I was always helping MK make beaded friendship bracelets. So, if he got that I was gay from that, then he had some serious fucking issues because I could have very well not have been gay and just liked to play with my sisters. I realized it was never anything that I said or did to make him come after me as much and as often as he did; it was his own prejudice and fears. I was always going to be this person, with or without his hateful behavior toward me. And that thought made me lift my head up and look at my friends who were staring at me, horrified. *Because I have nothing to be ashamed of.*

Jack sat up straighter. "He really put a gun to your head over me?"

I looked him in the eyes. "And pulled the trigger. I always told you that if my father ever found out about us, he would have put a bullet in me. You thought I was just saying that."

"Connor, I still can't believe you never told me how bad it was," he said sadly.

"I never told anyone. No one knew. Except Afia." I looked toward the door again.

"Well, he could have just done you a favor and told you when you were a kid. That way you could have told him to suck a bag of dicks and moved in with Jack's family," Brayden said, making us all laugh. "Then you two would have been happily ever after."

Ethan shoved him. "Then Jack and I wouldn't have been together, dumb ass."

"Oh yeah, right. When did you get here again?" Brayden asked jokingly, and Ethan shoved him again.

I was laughing and looked over at Jamel, who was also laughing but watching me. I could see the worry in his eyes for me. I really wished all these people weren't there, or that he would hold me. I just wanted to be in his arms.

Fuck it. I stood up and moved to stand in front of him. He didn't hesitate; he pushed his chair back and pulled me closer. I leaned over and kissed his lips softly and said, "I love you." Then I turned around and sat in his lap. He wrapped his arm around my waist, first putting his head on my back and breathing in my scent and rubbed his hands on my chest across my pecs, and then sat back but still held onto me. I lifted one hand to kiss, then laid it back across my stomach, and we laced our fingers. I looked around, and everyone was watching and smiling at us.

"What?" I asked casually.

Ethan answered, "Nothing. You're just..." He took a sip of his beer for dramatic effect and said, "Really fucking gay." Jamel laughed out loud, along with everyone else. Ethan continued, "I don't know how the fuck none of you saw it, and you all grew up with him."

I reached over and flicked his shoulder. "Asshole!" I said, as I laughed too.

Ethan laughed and shrugged his shoulders. "Hey, ain't nothing wrong with being really gay. I'm really gay too," he said and smiled at Jack.

Jack laughed and nodded vigorously. "Ethan is really, really fucking gay." We all laughed as he continued. "I don't know how he ended up married to a woman."

"Hey!" Mina said, feigning offense. "We aren't a bad species."

Ethan said, "Ain't nothing wrong with women, sweetheart; it's just that y'all don't have the equipment I want. I've been to the other side, and I like it here a lot better."

I held out my hand to Ethan for a slap, which he did. "A whole lot better," I agreed. "There's nothing like it."

Winter agreed. "Yeeesss honey, having a big strong man up against you, moving inside of you, hmmmm…" I held my hand out to her too, and she hit my palm and laughed.

Ethan laughed and said, "Yeah, Winter? That's why you got a baby now."

We laughed as she punched his arm. "It could have been yours," she said seductively to him.

He laughed again. "It would have never been mine."

"Give it up; Win, it's been twelve years. The man just told you he's super gay," Sam said.

"Whoa, I said *really* gay, I didn't say super gay," Ethan clarified. "Really gay is knowing that what you like, want, and need is a man, and make no apologies for it. Super gay is…" he snapped two fingers across his face flamboyantly, "…something totally different."

"Yes, please enlighten us on the ways of gaydom, Mr. My Bedroom is Private," Jamel said, teasing his friend.

"Right, and it still is," Ethan said, as if he was teaching a class. "I don't hide the fact that I'm gay; it's just none of your business who I'm sleeping with."

"You mean it's not our business how much you love cum in your mouth?" I said, just to see him blush.

And Ethan did, his face flushed pink. While our friends laughed, he looked over at Jack and smiled. Jack smiled back and took a sip of beer. "What the fuck do you two talk about when I'm not around?" Ethan asked.

"Your dick sucking skills, what else?" I said with a smirk. Jack spit out his beer, making everyone laugh louder and run for cover.

Ethan stood up. "Which by the way," he said loudly, over our roaring in laughter, "Is top fucking notch, since you want to be in *my* business!" This only made us laugh more.

EJ, Imani, and Freddie who were across the room looked up quizzically. I didn't know Imani was there until just then. Ethan yelled over to them, "Mind your business, kids! The grownups are talking!"

Jack walked up and kissed Ethan on the lips. Ethan hummed, then pulled him closer by his jet-black hair to stick his tongue down his throat. They kept kissing until Jamel started banging on the table, "Yo, get a fucking room, you queers!"

"Yo! Cock-sucking queers, thank you very much!" Ethan yelled out loud.

"C'mon, Dad, what the eff?" EJ yelled back across the room, embarrassed.

"Watch your fucking mouth!" he yelled back.

"What the hell kinda conversation are you queer-ass folks having over there?" Angie asked in amusement, also from the other side of the room. Deann was sitting with her.

But she never got the answer because the door burst open, and I heard her voice all panicky, "CONNOR!"

I turned to see my Lovie running toward me, with Ty, their children, and Kim right behind her. I stumbled off Jamel and met her halfway, lifting her off her feet, spinning her around. She was already crying and apologizing.

"I'm so sorry, I'm so sorry, I'm so sorry, I should have been there, I should have ... oh God, I'm so, so sorry!"

And me saying, "It's okay, it's okay. It was better this way."

Because if Afia was there, she would have dragged me out of there by my ear first.

"Hi, Uncle Connor, Uncle Mel," Kim said, as she rushed past us to get to her friends. She went straight to Freddie, holding onto him tightly. Kim hugged the other two, then sat down in the corner with them, and the four of them huddled. I'm guessing the topic was how I tried to kill his dad.

"Are you okay, for real?" Afia asked in my chest. She didn't let me answer before she pulled back, grabbing my face and looking me in the eyes, saying coldly, "You should have murdered that sonofabtich!"

I heard Jamel laugh loudly at that. She stormed over to him and swatted his arm. "YOU! How could you let it get that far? Have I taught you nothing!? If you don't get him out of there early, this is what happens!"

"Ow!" he cried, pretending that she actually hurt him. "I tried, but it was too late! Matty's mouth was like liquid diarrhea."

"It really was," Brayden agreed. "We came into the room the first time he swung on Connor. It was like he was asking for it."

Ty went over to his brother and gave him a dap. I heard him say to Jamel, "Sorry. Afia needed to detach so we were in the park with the girls, and neither of us had our phones. Kim was sitting on our porch waiting for us. She told us everything Freddie and EJ told her. You good, man?"

Jamel did not give him a verbal response. When I got closer to them, Ty turned around to face me. I gave him a head nod, but he pulled me in for a hug, and hugging was something we never do.

"I'm sorry, man. I heard all the things he said to you. About your father and the abuse? Your family is fucked up."

I nodded, lost for words with Ty at first. I ended up mumbling, "I tried to tell you all those years ago."

Ty shrugged. "Then he deserved what he got. From Jack, me, and you." He looked me in the eyes and said, "No regrets, okay?" I nodded, and he patted me on the back. It was kind. And brotherly.

He and Lovie sat down, and I resumed sitting on Jamel's lap. She said again, "I should have been there. Calling me a nigger bitch. This nigger bitch would have scratched his fucking eyes out," she snarled.

I chuckled. "Calm down, Lovie, I wouldn't have let you. I didn't let Jamel or Jack do it either. It had to be me."

"Would you really have killed him?" Sam asked in a hushed voice. "Because I'm not going to lie, we all thought you were."

I didn't answer but Jack did. "In a fucking heart-beat. And we would have all said it was self-defense when the cops showed up." He looked around, daring anyone to dispute that. Brayden and Sam did not. I looked over at him and gave him a slight head nod. He nodded back.

"Angie saved his life," said Jack.

"No. Angie saved Connor's life," Jamel said. "She didn't do it for Matty. If it was you with a tie around his neck, Jack, she probably would have let you kill him. You got a rich suga daddy, but going to prison for murder a second time wouldn't look good on my husband's resume."

A couple of us chuckled, including me. But then Jamel said seriously, "It's the same reason I took the gun from his hands the night Owen came to our house. It's not that he couldn't do it. It's that even-tually knowing that he did would have destroyed him. Connor has been through enough."

I smiled as he held me tighter. Winter asked, "So what now? You have two of his kids here with you. You're still connected through your mother and sis-ters. It was bad before but... How are y'all supposed to function around each other now?"

I had no idea. I glanced over at Freddie with his friends and then at Deann playing with Evie, sitting with her aunts and uncles.

"That's tomorrow's problem," Jamel answered for me. "Today, Connor takes care of himself."

CHAPTER 12

SCARED, BUT LIGHTER.
BETTER. FREE.

Connor

It turned into a kind of gathering of my friends, and BJ never made it back to the inn. Someone started music, and we sang and danced together. Then I heard it, the first chords of the song that brought me back to my dream. I screamed over the chatter, "Shut up, shut up, shut up, everybody shut the fuck up!"

They all turned to look at me, and I was able to hear the song that Vinnie was singing to me. Jamel looked at me confused, but instead of answering, I just started singing the song by Lauv, "Sad Forever." I stood up, closed my eyes, and started spinning. I felt soft hands around me and, at first, I thought it was Afia, but then I heard my baby sister's voice. Angie wrapped her arms around me and sang with me too. And it hit me; that was the line Vinnie was singing to me over and over again. He was warning me that this was coming, but I was going to make it through to the other side. And I wouldn't be sad forever. I wouldn't be sad anymore. I held back tears as I danced and sang with my baby sister.

The song went off, and I turned to Angie and hugged her. I began to feel incredibly guilty. I started, "I'm sorry—"

But she cut me off. "Don't. Don't apologize. Not to me."

"Then I should be thanking you. For not letting it happen."

"It was a hard decision. Hard as fuck," she said coldly. Then she smiled and I laughed. She really was so much like me.

Mary Kate came up behind me and hugged me. I turned around and pulled her close, and the three of us hugged. It dawned on me that MK chose to follow me instead of staying with Matty, and that warmed my heart.

"I'm sorry, Mini Kat," I said to her. "I know you love your brother."

"I do," she said and looked up at me. "Both my brothers. I love you too. What he did to you was unforgivable, and I'll never defend him again. Even his own children knew it and walked out on him."

I looked over at Deann and said, "You walked out too?"

"Well, I had to. They said they didn't want me there either," she said to me, but avoided my eyes. I looked at her quizzically. "You didn't hear what happened?"

"Noooo… What happened?"

She took a deep breath. "So, you know my best friend, Mackenzie?"

I heard Jamel's voice behind me. "Don't bother explaining, we already know that she's your girlfriend, Dee."

Her eyes went wide. "Oh fuck," she said, embarrassed.

I laughed, went over, and put my arm around her. "So, you're ready to come out?" I asked her gently.

Mary Kate laughed and told me, "She kinda already did."

Angie said, "Yeah, kinda reminiscent of when you came out. Remember how you yelled at Mom, 'I'm gaaaaay!'? Yeah, it was like that."

"Holy shit!" I hugged her tighter. "Are you okay? How do you feel?"

"Scared, but lighter. Better. Free."

I nodded at her. "Yeah, me too." She grinned. "Well, you're eighteen now so, fuck it. You'll just move in with me."

"That's what Freddie told her," Jamel said. "He just offered up our basement."

I laughed. "That fucking kid of mine." I looked around, and I didn't see him or EJ, Kim, and Imani anymore. "Where is he?"

"He was right … there…" Jamel looked around too, then looked at me, puzzled. He called over to Ethan, "Hey E, where's EJ and Fred?"

Ethan sighed and came over to us. "They left about an hour ago. Freddie asked if he could stay at our house tonight. I think…" He looked at me. "For some reason he's blaming himself for all that happened. Something about the tie. Do you know what he means?"

Jamel and I exchanged glances. Ethan continued. "He thinks you might be mad at him or wouldn't want to be around him because he gave you the idea about the tie. I told him he could stay if he wanted. They're across the street at the house."

"I'll go talk to him," I said to Jamel.

I put on my shoes and crossed the street to ring the doorbell, then turned the knob. The four of them were sitting on the couch, watching a show. Freddie, who was holding hands with Kim, looked at me all wide-eyed but stood up.

"Hey, Uncle Con," he said cautiously.

"Can we talk? Alone?" I asked.

"We'll head back over," Imani said. She grabbed EJ before he could say anything and pulled him out the door. Kim gave him one last hug, then hugged me too on her way out.

When it closed, I sat down on the couch. Freddie sighed and sat down next to me. I told him, "I'm sorry you had to see me like that. I'm sorry you almost lost your dad today. My brother and I have a long and bad history, but sometimes I forget that he's your father too. I would never want to harm someone that you love."

"I was scared, for sure," he said. "I thought you were going to do it too. And I thought … this sounds fucked up. But a part of me thought that you'd do it and then I'd get to live with you full time. But then I thought you'd go to jail, and then I'd lose you too. Then I felt bad about wanting my father to die. I didn't really want him to die but…" He took a moment, then asked, "Did you do it for me? Did you put the tie around his neck for me?"

I looked into his worried eyes. "No," I lied. "I wasn't thinking, that's all. I was reacting out of anger, hurt, and pain. Pain that was inflicted on me by my own father, that for some reason your father wanted to bring up and attack me with. Because I was in emotional pain, I almost did a really bad thing and inflicted physical pain, and it would have hurt a lot of people, including you. I'm truly sorry for that. Like I always tell you, you don't want to be like me. Think before you do things."

"Yeah but…" He looked thoughtful. "What's going to happen now? Because I don't want to go back. And I know Deann's not going back. Can't I just stay with you? Because he's going to hurt me again, just like Grandpa did to you. You're stronger than me; I won't be able to handle it. Please, Uncle Connor, I'll be fifteen soon; I can make my own decisions."

My heart was breaking. I wanted so badly to just tell him yes. That I would take care of him, raise him like my own son, maybe even adopt him, and make him mine. But I knew that wasn't possible.

"Freddie, I'm not your legal guardian, and I can't give you permission to live with me," I said and watched his face fall in disappointment. "But listen to me. No matter what happens between your dad and I, I will never, ever turn my back on you. My home will always be your home. And you know Jamel feels the same way. If anything were to ever happen to me, like going to jail or something, he'll take care of you."

He had tears in his eyes and said again to me, "I don't want to go back." I pulled him in for a hug and he cried on my chest. "What's gonna happen tomorrow?"

I told him, "You don't have to go back tonight. They know where you are. We'll worry about tomorrow's problems tomorrow."

When we walked back into the Inn, my mother was standing there with my sisters, still in her black dress. Waiting for me. The guilt hit me like a ton of bricks. I tried to kill my mother's son, the one she had to revive back to life. The one her own husband also tried to kill twice. How was I different from Owen?

I started walking to her but then stopped. I didn't know what to say. She closed the gap by walking to me and reached up and touched my cheek gently. That's when the tears began to fall out of my eyes, the first time I cried all day. All week.

"I'm sorry," I mouthed to her.

She gave me a small smile. "Matthew is okay," she said. "Henry called the ambulance, and they took him to Providence General. Stephanie, Madeline, and BJ are with him. He has a crushed larynx, a broken nose, and a fractured leg bone. He will need surgery and be in the hospital for a long while, but he will live." There was a hush, so I knew everyone was listening.

My mother took both my hands and said, "I told him and Stephanie if he presses charges, I will cut him out of my life for good. I will not go through another trial, tearing this family apart. Matthew is not the head of this family; I am."

I nodded. She turned around, still holding onto my hand and addressed the room. "I'm sorry you all had to witness that. But it had been brewing for years between my sons. And my late husband was the cause of this friction."

She took a moment, then said, "I want to thank you all for standing by my sweet boy. For being his family all of these years when we weren't. Afia and Jack, you two especially. He survived all he survived because of the two of you."

She looked around and found my husband's face. "Jamel, I've never officially thanked you for the way you've taken care of Connor all these years. The way you love him, stand by him, held him up when we didn't, it means the world to me as his mother. And the way you've just embraced and love my grandchildren, despite who their father is… You're a good man. Eleven years too late, but you need to know, I am so grateful for you. And I am so happy and honored to call you my son, and to have you a part of my life and my family."

"Thanks … Mom," he said quietly. I saw Jamel's face. He tried to hide it, but it meant the world to him for my mother to say these things to him, and publicly at that.

She looked around and spotted my niece. "Deann, you'll stay with me. You and Freddie."

Freddie protested, "I wanna stay with Uncle Connor!"

"Fredrick." My mother called his name warningly over her shoulder. He didn't say anything else.

She turned back to me and touched my face again. "I love you, Connor. I am so sorry I didn't protect you all those years. But I have always loved you, just the way you are. My loving, beautiful, strong, amazing, gay son."

Even though she had always accepted me, it was the first time she publicly acknowledged me as a gay man. And it made me cry again. She pulled me close and hugged me. My sisters came around, and The McIntyres hugged together.

My mother left with Freddie and Deann while Angie, Chad, and the kids went back to my house, and Mary Kate and Dennis went to the hospital to see Matty. Sam, Mina, and Winter left together to go back to the Jennings residence. Afia and Ty stayed awhile, but they had to leave to drop off Imani and Kim, and Brayden took EJ to his grandmother's house after Imani left. So, it ended up being just the four of us.

The sound system in the dining room continued to play random songs from Amazon Music. Jack broke out the whiskey and said, "Get fucked up and stay in the Inn tonight. Consider it a late anniversary gift."

We took him up on the offer and went through a whole bottle, talking and laughing. Jamel had taken my chair and stretched his legs out on me, while Jack and Ethan sat side by side, Jack leaning on Ethan's shoulder.

Ethan asked, "Do you think Matty's going to do it? Press charges?"

I shrugged. "I don't know. He just might, despite my mother's threat."

"Well like I said, if he does, there are at least eight to ten people who will testify that he hit you first. After he yelled racial and homophobic slurs. Ain't that right, Jamel?" said Jack.

"That's what I saw," said my husband.

I smiled a little. "Well, at least I know if I go to prison, Jamel will be in good hands." I looked over and winked at him, and he laughed out loud.

"I don't get it," Jack said.

"Oh, you mean with us?" Ethan asked. "Of course, Jamel is my boy; we'll definitely look out for him."

Jamel and I started giggling. Ethan and Jack looked at each other confused, which only made us laugh harder. "Alright, no more whiskey for you," Ethan said, moving my cup to the side.

"No, it's just that…" I was talking while laughing. "We kinda made a pact … so you know… You should probably know too … since it concerns you…"

"What kind of pact?" Jack asked, as his eyes narrowed.

I looked at Jamel and started laughing again, so he answered. "We just said that if something were to happen to one of you, we would take the other one in. Like a throuple."

"A polyamorous triad!" I yelled, happy I had that knowledge.

Jack sat all the way up and Ethan said, "What the fuck?"

This made Jamel and I laugh harder. "So, it's only fair…" I continued in my fit of laughter while talking, "that if something were to happen to one of us … you'd take the other one too."

"Oh God, the look on your face, E," Jamel said in between his laughter.

Jack looked at Ethan and started laughing too. "You look horrified."

The three of us were laughing as Ethan was taking it all in and eventually started chuckling. "Fuck. No. You two are fucking crazy."

"Seeeeee, I told you Ethan wouldn't take care of meeeeee," I whined to Jamel.

"C'mon man, you're making me look bad," Jamel said in amusement. "I told him you would take care of him for me, that you'd do it for me if I asked you to."

Jack started laughing harder. "Who thinks of shit like this?"

"People who know their partner won't be able to survive without them," I said. I turned to my baby and put my hand on his neck, saying, "I can't live without Jamel." We stared at each other lovingly.

"Oh, fuck. Okay, we'll take you in," Ethan said fatherly and motioning with his hands to come over. "But you can't fuck Jack. You'll be a full bottom and get fucked by both of us. That's the rule."

Jack and Jamel burst out in laughter, but I reached over for a handshake. "Deal." Then I thought about it. "But wait, what if I go first, then what happens with Mel?"

"Same rules apply," Ethan said, then started laughing.

"Fuck you, nobody is dicking me!" Jamel yelled and laughed.

"Well then find yourself another throuple then, shit!" Ethan laughed.

We were all laughing when Jack said to Jamel, "It's okay, you can fuck me."

I gasped; my eyes opened as wide as Ethan's, and he pushed Jack onto the floor. "Get the fuck outta here!"

"Oh, don't act like you wouldn't be happy fucking Connor!" Jack said from the ground. "Remember when you told me that he has a great ass?"

My mouth dropped as Ethan kicked his husband playfully. Jamel was as shocked as I was. "Yeah, E? You're checking out my husband's ass?" he asked amusingly.

Ethan waved his hand dismissively. "That's common knowledge. Everyone in New England knows Connor has a great ass. Shit, I'm the only one in this room that hasn't tapped it!"

That made us all laugh hysterically. I fell forward laughing as Jack exclaimed, "Holy shit!" laughing from the floor. Jamel pinched my butt, making me yelp and laugh some more.

Jack crawled back up into Ethan's lap and straddled him. He tried to kiss him, but Ethan kept moving his face around, avoiding it. "Nah son, you just gave away my ass, like it was yours to give, nah. Not cool, man. Not cool."

"Eeeeethaaaan," Jack whined out his name, as he threw his arms around his neck. "I love you," we heard him say, barely above a whisper.

"More than you'll ever know," Ethan said back softly, rubbing his back.

He held Jack's face up. They stared at each other lovingly for a moment as we watched them. Then Ethan leaned to the right, looking beyond Jack at us, and asked, "If something were to happen to me, you'd take care of my Jackie Bear?"

"Only if we get to call him Jackie Bear," I teased.

"Fuck off," Jack said without turning around, and I laughed.

"No question, E. We got him," Jamel said seriously. "The kids too."

He gave a simple shrug. "Then we got Connor."

Jamel raised his glass to his friend. I turned to my husband, and he winked at me.

❤

As soon as the door closed in Room 3, I pounced.

Jamel was walking in front of me, and I pulled him back by his shirt and put my fingers under it, running my hands across his hairy chest and bit him on the back of his neck. He turned around and we kissed hungrily. I lifted off his shirt, then my tank top and pulled him closer, biting his lip as we kissed, sucking his tongue with force. He moaned in his throat and grabbed me by my bottom. I put my arms around his neck and lifted my feet as he picked me up. He rarely carried me like that because I hated feeling like the female in our relationship, but Jamel was strong and his strength was everything I needed at the moment, and he knew it.

Jamel turned around and carried me to the bed and gently laid me down. He kissed me all over from my neck to the top of my groin area, then undid my pants and pulled them down, taking my boxer briefs with them. He ended up on his knees and pulled me closer to him, his face in my naked crotch, rubbing his cheek against my penis over and over again. I rubbed my hands all over his head as I felt his tongue join the party. I was sweaty and musty, neither of us had showered since that morning, but he didn't care, and I certainly didn't.

He put his mouth on my cock head and I moaned out loud, then I thrusted up and shoved the rest down his throat. Jamel rarely gags, but he did that time because it was unexpected. I did it again and again, essentially keeping his head steady while I fucked his mouth and he played with my balls. I didn't stop until my midsection froze up and I came in his mouth, and Jamel dutifully swallowed every drop of me. That feeling of sweet release was ecstasy, like I had been holding back for the last couple of hours since the tie snapped.

And now I need to get fucked. Hard.

He lifted his head up and looked at me, lovingly. I could tell he wanted to make love but that was not what I wanted. I moved back on the bed. He went into the bathroom and came back out naked and with the little bottle of complimentary lotion, since we had no lube on us. He crawled over me, kissing my body as he made his way up—my legs and calves, the inside of my thighs, my leaking penis, the V part of my groin, my chest. Then he switched to his tongue and licked my nipples, biting them a little. He licked the sweat off my neck and put his tongue in my ear, making me moan. My dick started getting hard again up against his already swollen cock.

Jamel leaned in close to my face. He kissed me softly, nuzzled his nose with mine, then kissed me softly again. "Fuck me, Big Daddy," I said to him seductively.

He smiled at me. Then he turned me on my side, putting my leg at an angle. He used the lotion, putting it onto his fingers and pushing it inside of me, rubbing around, making my inside moist. He spit on his own hands and mixed it with the lotion to stroke himself. Then he entered me, slowly. I relaxed my body and took all of him in. When he bottomed out, he kissed me, but I turned my face away first and moved my body against him. He got the hint and started to move too. But he moved slow and steady, the pace of sensuality and love. I moved faster against him as he kissed my neck and pinched my nipples.

"Fuck me. Harder. Harder," I demanded.

Jamel ignored me. He pushed me gently onto my stomach. He moved faster but not harder. He thrusted but not pounded. He touched me and kissed me, and I hated it. He was giving me what I needed but not what I wanted. I did not want to feel loved. I did not want to feel at all.

"Please Jamel, please." I pleaded with him. "Please, I can't feel this right now … I can't."

He lifted me up just enough so he could wrap both arms around my chest and said a quiet, "No."

He made love to me, intentionally. He moved in and out of me like silk. He left soft, wet kisses all over my neck and back. He rubbed his hands all over me, through my close-cropped hair, down my arms to lace his fingers with mine. He showed me how deeply he loved me, and I was on the verge of tears. It was too much.

"Please, baby," I cried out. "I can't ... I can't ... just fuck me."

Jamel pulled out slowly and turned me to my back. He leaned all the way on me, his cock against mine. He kissed my lips and my face and said, in my ear, "I know what you want. You want to feel physical pain to avoid the emotional one. But you need to know you are loved, Connor. You said whatever happens today, you want to feel all of it. And you did: the fear, frustration, acceptance, rage, guilt, shame. Now feel this. Let me love you, baby. Let me love you."

I couldn't stop it. The tears started flowing like a dam had burst. My breathing became labored, and I started wailing as if I was in pain. Everything just hurt so fucking bad.

Jamel scooped me up in his arms and held me tight. I grabbed him tightly back, and he let me cry and wail. I even screamed at one point. Through it all, he never let me go.

When my crying subsided to whimpering, only then did he lift up, add more lotion to me, and enter me again. He moved my legs to the sides of him and watched me as he sexed me deeply. I held onto his arms, tears flowing down the side of my face as I got lost and drowned in his gray eyes. He would lean down to wipe them away, kiss me from time to time. I don't know how long we stayed that way, but eventually I was close, and I knew he was too.

"I'm gonna cum," he told me.

"I'm cumming too," I moaned out.

I moved one hand to my member and began stroking upwards while he thrusted into me, pulled back, then thrusted again. He continued to do so until he drew out my name in that way that he still does, "Cooooonoooor..." and the moment I felt my cum rush through me was the same moment I felt his rush inside of me. He filled me up while I ejaculated on both of us, and we came at exactly the same time. We moaned together our exaltation, then he collapsed on me. We stayed this way, me rubbing the sweat down his spine with my fingertips, our heartbeats slowing down together. Then he leaned up and kissed me slowly, sensually as he slid out of me.

He went to the bathroom, then came back to the bed and wiped me down with a warm, wet cloth. I watched him until he was done, then he laid down on his side, and I turned to him.

"Jamel." I called his name, but I didn't have words.

It didn't matter because he understood my heart. He looked at me for a moment and nodded slowly. "I'm here for you. Always."

Then he nuzzled his nose with mine, kissed the tip of my nose, and pulled me close to where my head was on his chest. I don't know who fell asleep first.

When I woke up, he was still sleeping on his side. I was laying on his arm, my hands clasped together in front of me, and his other hand was across my waist. I stared at him, his dark brown skin, his thin beard and mustache, full lips and wide nose, thick hairy eyebrows, curvy small ears, pronounced Adam's apple. Same dark Caesar haircut he had when we first met.

Still the most beautiful man in the world to me. Still the most loving, caring, attentive, affectionate, gentlest man I've ever known. And he's still in love with me.

CHAPTER 13

I GET ANGRY

Jamel

I t's not something I think about, but it had always been
in the back of my mind that Connor would cheat on
me one day. Connor valued his sexual freedom when
we first met, and I was worried he would feel trapped
by being with just me sexually. Maybe that was why I
wanted to do the threesome. Besides the fact that I'd
always been curious about who Connor was before
me, that sexual predator side, maybe a part of me
believed that if he did it with me, it would postpone
the inevitable. When I met him, he was promiscuous,
and you don't just go from fucking different people
to one person for the rest of your life overnight. And
the truth was, I already forgave him for it, whether it
happened in the next year or twenty years from now.
Nick told me that. When Connor and I first started
dating, he told me that if I really loved him, I had to

accept the fact that one day he just might sleep with someone else and to be ready to forgive him for it immediately. And if it never happened, then it would be a happy surprise. Either way, when I told him I would never leave him, I meant it.

At the same time, we've never had a situation where I actively worried about it, until now. Every time I saw that asshole Nate subtly flirting with him, it bothered me. A lot. I really fucking hated that guy. Nate was exactly the type of guy that I always pictured Connor cheating on me with: white, same build, arguably a little handsome. A Marine just like him. Connor thought it was the same as his hatred for the sanitation man. But Connor also knew my past, knew I had been cheated on by the ones I've loved and knew I would never do it to someone else, especially not to him. It's just not the same, because the potential to cheat wasn't in me. I tried not to hold his history against him, but sex and love were two very different things for him for a very long time. I'm the only person, besides Vinnie, that had really given him one in the same.

I would like to believe that it's enough, but I'm a realist. So, if it does happen, I'll be hurt and upset, but I'll forgive him the one time. But the other guy won't get the same courtesy. Especially if it's Nate fucking Proctor.

Ethan asked me to check on the circuit breaker so instead of coming into Connor's office from the leasing door like I usually do, I came up through the basement of the apartment building and made my way to the entrance from inside the building that the residents use. The door was ajar, and I heard them, heard *him* say, "It makes me feel better to know that."

"You just have to have faith," Connor told him. "Faith that it will all work out in the end. Faith that you'll find…"

But Connor trailed off as I came closer and glanced in. They were sitting on his desk side by side. Nate was slowly trailing the back of his fingers down Connor's bare arm. Connor watched his fingers as Nate said, "I'm not looking for love; I just want a reason to feel alive again."

My heart stopped as Connor looked up at him. I held my breath as Nate leaned in. But Connor leaned back slightly and said calmly, "What the fuck are you doing, Nathaniel?"

Nate leaned back and apologized, "I'm sorry, Connor. I didn't mean to make you uncomfortable."

"Yes. You did," Connor responded. "You've been wanting to make me uncomfortable for months now. Especially in the last couple of weeks, ever since you found out my father died. Maybe you thought it would finally make me vulnerable and I would need a shoulder to cry on, or a cock to suck to make me feel better. Our fucked up fathers giving us a shared history. Is that what you thought?"

"Is that so bad?" Nate asked softly.

Connor stood up with his back to the door so I couldn't see his facial expression. "No. It's not bad if it's for someone who wants what you want. But that's not me. And you already knew that, but you tried anyway. Why?"

Nate sighed and put his hands between his legs. "I just thought maybe you'd give it a chance."

Connor scoffed. "I'm fucking married. And even if I wasn't, what you need is a trusting friend, not for me to put my dick in your ass."

Nate raised his hands up in surrender. "Okay, okay. I'm sorry. Really and truly." He stood up, and I moved to the side of the door and leaned my back against the wall so they wouldn't see me. I heard Nate say, "I won't do it again."

"No, you won't," Connor said plainly. "Because you're not allowed to come back in here unless it's building-related. Now get the fuck out of my office."

Nate made it to the door, then turned around and said, "I meant no disrespect to you or your marriage. I'll respect your boundaries."

"That's all I ask," I heard Connor say.

Nate passed me by, oblivious of me standing there, as he made his way to his apartment. I whistled to get his attention. He turned around, and his eyes went wide for a second as I startled him.

"Hey Nate, do me a favor?" I said calmly, as I walked toward him. "Keep your fucking hands off my husband."

His mouth opened slightly, then he smirked and said, "For sure. Until he tells me otherwise."

"Or until I snap your neck. Whatever comes first. Guess which one is coming first?" I gave him an icy cold glare, as I came closer and his cocky smile faded.

Connor appeared in the doorway. "Jamel?"

I stopped walking, but I didn't look at him. I still had my eyes on that asshole, who slithered away into his apartment.

Connor called my name again. "Jamel? What the fuck?"

I looked at him, and I wanted to snap the fuck out. While I was elated that Connor shut him down, not just out of respect for our relationship but for himself, the majority of me was pissed off. I told him not to let Nate get close to him. I warned him that he was not innocent. But Connor just had to handle shit on his own and let it get this far. I was so mad; I felt my anger filling up my chest like lead.

"Fuck this shit," I said angrily. I turned away from him and walked back out of the building.

"Jamel!" Connor yelled my name.

I kept going. I got into my truck and drove home, angry as fuck. Angry at Connor for not listening to me in the first place. Angry at myself for not beating the shit out of Nate. Angry that the one person I wanted to call and vent to was fucking dead.

I drove like Connor drives, fast and reckless. I kept one hand on the wheel and called Ethan. The phone rang a few times, then went to voicemail.

"*Hey, this is Ethan, leave me a message and I'll call you back.*"

I screamed into the phone. "Fuck, Ethan! Pick up the goddamn phone! You better call me back before I murder that sonofabitch in your building. That motherfucker put his fucking hands on my fucking husband, and I swear to God, I swear to fucking God if he fucks him ... somebody is going to stop fucking breathing! You better—"

But the line beeped again and cut me off. "FUCK!"

I called Henry next but it went straight to message too. I didn't bother hollering on his voicemail. I just kept driving, running stop signs and barely catching red lights. I pulled into my garage and sat there a moment to catch my breath. Less than a minute later, Connor's white 4Runner pulled in right behind me, and honestly it was the last thing I needed. I needed to feel what I felt without having to monitor his feelings too. I got out of the car and went inside through the garage into the house without looking at him.

"Jamel, what the fuck!" Connor yelled at me through his car window.

I ignored him, went upstairs into the kitchen, and poured a glass of Hennessy. I finished the first glass in one motion, poured a second and gulped much of that down. I had to find a way to calm down, but nothing was working. I felt like punching a wall. A wall named Nate fucking Proctor.

By the time Connor came upstairs, I was leaning against the island in the kitchen, calmly sipping. He looked at me and said angrily, "What the fuck was that?"

"You don't know what that was?" I said quietly, the complete opposite of what I felt.

"I told you to let me handle it."

"Yeah, I saw how well you handled it."

"Yeah. I did. Without threatening to snap his fucking neck."

I didn't respond because my comment wasn't meant as a compliment. He fucked this shit up in a major way because he didn't put a cork in it from day one. *And now I have to deal with him working in close proximity to someone who made it clear he wants to fuck him. I'm fucking pissed.*

He kept reprimanding me. "Are you insane? Since when did you become this person? Threatening someone, driving like a fucking maniac, not to mention snapping at me, saying fuck this shit? Fuck what shit, this? *Us??* What the fuck! Why are you acting like—"

"Like you?" I cut him off, speaking a little louder than intended.

He scoffed. "I don't act like that."

I laughed sarcastically. "Yeah, okay." I gulped the rest of my drink, poured another glass, and walked out of the kitchen.

Connor followed me and said, "And even if I do act like that once in a blue, *you* don't. So again, what the fuck was that?" Again, I didn't answer as I paced my living room. "Nate asked me in the beginning if he should be afraid of you and I told him no, that you don't fuck people up, I do. Clearly that was a fucking lie."

I stopped pacing and glared at him. "Wait, what? You told him *not* to be afraid of me? Why the fuck did you do that?"

He threw his hands out. "Because I didn't want him to think you were the angry Black man. But you sure proved that shit wrong today!"

"So Black men aren't allowed to be angry?" I asked calmly, taking a sip of my liquor.

"What? I didn't say that!"

"Because Black men, just like white men and Latino men and Asian men, get angry all the time. We're allowed to be human."

"I didn't say you can't be angry, Mel. I just didn't want him assuming that you would come after him!" he yelled at me.

"But I *will* come after him, Connor," I said calmly and dangerously. "I will pistol whip the shit out of him if he touches you again. And if he fucks you or you fuck him, I'm *going* to snap his fucking neck."

I threw my head back to finish my drink, turned around, and threw the glass against the dining room wall, and it shattered into pieces. I turned back to Connor's shocked face, his mouth practically on the floor.

"I get angry," I said quietly.

I started walking away, but he grabbed my arm. "Who the fuck are you right now!?"

"Let. Me. Go."

He moved to stand in front of me. "And if I don't, you're gonna pistol whip the shit out of me too?"

I scoffed at him and pulled my arm from his grasp. "Get out of my way. I need to take a shower."

"Fuck no!" Connor yelled. "You don't get to do that! You don't get to be a complete asshole and then walk away from me like you didn't just say the shit you just said. If you can't trust me to handle shit my way, or even worse, *to not fuck somebody else*, then what the fuck are we doing here!?"

I'm going to flip the fuck out if he doesn't stop talking.

"Connor—" I tried but he cut me off.

"I'm so sick of this shit! I don't even know who the fuck I'm married to anymore!"

"Connor—"

He was still yelling at me. "I got my own shit that I'm dealing with! My father died! My dog died! I almost killed my fucking brother! We all have problems, but I'm dealing with mine. That last thing I need is for you to change on me because you can't fucking deal with yours."

"Connor." I gritted my teeth.

"Because I swear to God, Mel, if this keeps going the way it's going, then fuck this shit because I'm not stayin—"

"CONNOR, SHUT THE FUCK UP! SHUT. THE. FUCK. UP!"

His mouth dropped to the floor again, and it's because I had never screamed at him before. Ever.

But fuck it. It's my turn to go the fuck off, for once.

"Guess what!?" I yelled. "My fucking dog died too! And you're not the only one that lost someone! I couldn't even pick up the phone to tell my best friend what a dickhead my husband is being, because he's DEAD! So yeah, we all have problems, but you get to deal with yours by putting all your emotional shit on ME! So, I don't get to *feel* things, because we can't be two emotional fag queens in here! There is only room for one, and shit, you take the fucking crown!"

His body jolted in indignation. "Holy shit! I am not an emotional fag queen!"

I laughed sarcastically again and threw my hands up in disbelief. "Connor, you are whiny, moody, immature, sensitive-ass, emotional-ass Cancer! Who the FUCK needs kids when I'm already raising a fucking teenager!?"

Connor put his hand to his chest all dramatic, like we were in a Turner Classic Movie film. "Fuck you, Mel! And you're a stubborn, pushy, jealous, closed-up, controlling Scorpio! And an asshole!"

"I gotta be, dealing with your ass!"

"Fuck you!" he screamed at me again. "If you don't want to be with me anymore, than just fucking go!"

Ugh, I can't take it!

I ran my hands over my face and yelled, "Fuck, Connor, stop saying that shit! It's so stupid, and I'm sick to death of you telling me to go or threatening to leave. You're not going any fucking where! Neither am I! Stop saying 'fuck this shit,' or 'I can't do this shit', or 'I'm not staying for this shit,' because YES THE FUCK YOU ARE!" For the third time, his mouth dropped in shock.

"Just because we have a fucking argument doesn't mean it's the end of us! But the thing is, you know that, *you fucking know that,* and yet you still say that shit! Stop it, goddammit! And while we're at it, stop asking me not to leave you! Leave and go where, to another emotionally immature asshole!? No, I'm kind of sold on the one I got, so how about *you* suck *that* shit up! So I threatened to snap someone's neck and threw a glass against the wall one time, and you're ready to sign divorce papers? Shut the fuck up with that dumb shit! Nobody is leaving, asshole!"

We stared at each other, his face in shock, my face angry. Then he started to giggle. He kept giggling that silly giggle he does, and it was getting harder for me not to laugh with him, although I had no idea what he was laughing about.

"I'm an emotional fag queen?" Connor started out-right laughing, and I accidentally smirked. He went into the kitchen, still laughing, then grabbed a glass, and hurled it at me. I ducked, and it smashed against the living room wall. He threw another one.

"What the fuck, Connor?"

"Well honey," he said in the most flamboyant voice he'd ever used, sounding like Emmitt from his show, *Queer as Folk*. "If I'm the emotional fag queen of this relationship, then I might as well play my fucking role."

Ah fuck.

He threw a third glass at my head. "Stop that shit!" I yelled at him.

"Why? I'm an immature fucking teenager, right?" he said amusingly. He went into the dining room and kicked one of the chairs so hard, poor Maje went running. He kicked a second one.

"Connor," I said warningly.

"WHAT!?" he yelled.

"You're going to clean this shit up!" I yelled at him.

"Fuck you, Sergeant! My daddy is dead, and you don't get to tell me what to do!"

"Connor!"

This motherfucker ran to the living room and started jumping on the couch, Tom Cruise- style, while flailing his arms around. He sang, "I aaaaam an emotional-aaaaass, sensitive-aaaaass, moody-aaaaaass Caaaaaaaaanceeeeeeeeeer!"

"Get the fuck off my couch."

"No! Eyyyyyyyyye am an emotionaaaaaaaaal-ass, sensitiiiiiiive-ass, moooooooody-ass Caaaaaaancer!"

He continued to dance and sing on the couch, and I thought, *Well that's it, I finally broke my husband.*

I walked over and tried to grab his arms, but he was pulling away quickly, still singing, "Eyyyyyyyeee am an emotional-ass, sensitive-ass, moody-ass Caaaaaanceeeeeerrrrr!"

Finally, I wrapped my arms around his waist and lifted him off the couch while he continued to sing. I slid him down my body as he wrapped his arms around my neck. He sang it softly, "I aaaaam an emooootionaaaal-aasss, sensitiiiiiiive-aaaaass, moooooooody-aaaaass Caaaaaaanceeeeerrrrr."

"Fuck, I love you," I said softly to him.

"Yeah?" Connor asked softly back. "If I ask you not to leave me right now, are you going to, like, have a brain aneurysm?"

I chuckled. "I hate that you make me laugh when I'm so mad." Even though I wasn't mad anymore. I didn't even realize when I stopped being mad. Somewhere between him clutching his imaginary pearls and jumping on the couch.

"And I love everything about you," he said, rubbing the back of my neck. "Even when you're mad. Even when you become the angry Black man. Which is your right as a man to get angry. Even at me." He kissed my lips softly and said, "You were right. I'm sorry I didn't nip it in the bud earlier. And I'm really sorry you lost your dog. And your best friend."

I closed my eyes and pulled him close against me. "I need to be inside of you," I said in his ear.

"Why?" Connor asked. "So you can reclaim something that you never lost in the first place? So you can remind me who I belong to, even though no one else has ever had me like you do? And no one ever will?"

I smiled. *He thinks he knows me so well.* I lifted up to meet his eyes. "Yes."

"Well, the good thing about us emotional-ass Cancers is that we're also very loving, sensual, sexual beings that love to get fucked by jealous, pushy, controlling-ass Scorpios," he said as he undid my jeans.

"I'm sorry I said those things," I told him, as guilt washed over me for losing control and yelling at him.

"No, you're not," he told me, as he got on his knees. "It's the most direct you have been with me about your feelings in a long time. You should flip out on me more often."

Connor put his mouth on my cock and bobbed his head a few times. "It was also the sexiest thing you've ever done, threatening to snap a man's neck for me."

He bobbed his head a few more times with that perfect suction he has. "Now tell me how it makes you feel when I suck your cock."

He deep-throated and held it there. I closed my eyes and moaned out, "Fuuuuck, you're a good little cocksucker."

I thought he gagged, but he pulled off laughing. "Holy shit, say that again."

He plunged back down, taking all of me in. "Uuuuugh, keep going, my good, little cocksucking lover."

He hummed on my dick, then began stroking his tongue against it up and down, making me moan loudly again. He came off and jerked me while he asked, "Hmmmm … you like the way I blow on this dick?"

"Love it," I breathed out. "Ten points. You get the gold medal every single time."

He gagged and left slimy spit on my cock. "Yeah? Olympic goal medal for dick- sucking?"

"Uuugh, among … other things."

Connor giggled and stood up. He kissed me and asked, "What other events do I get the gold for?"

I kissed his neck, and he giggled again while he started removing his belt. "Dick-riding, definitely." I sucked on his earlobe as he moaned. "Hand jobs." I moved his hand away and put my hand between his legs and grabbed his dick roughly. He moaned again. "How flexible you are." I zipped down his jeans and put my hand down his pants and he moaned again. "That tight, tight hole you have." I put my tongue in his mouth, making him moan a fourth time.

"Hmmm … you want to feel this tight, tight hole?"

"Yes. Right now. Right the fuck now."

He laughed, then went into the kitchen as I kicked off my jeans and underwear. He came back with olive oil, our lube of choice when we were downstairs, and got on his knees again. He poured oil on his hands and massaged my dick, giving me a hand job just as good as his blow job until the skin was tight, and I was leaking pre-cum.

"Tell me what you want," he said, as he stood up and dropped his pants.

"Wanna ride this cock?" I asked.

"Well if you're gonna be pushy about it…" he joked.

Asshole. I changed my mind. I took the oil from his hands, and I pushed him toward the wall next to the front door. I put a ridiculous amount of oil on my fingers and inserted them all the way inside his anus until I felt his nub. He moaned my name loudly. I did it three more times until he was nice and silky, then I grinded against his ass over and over again, sliding my cock right along that perfect crack of his. I bit that space between his neck and his shoulder, and he yelped.

"Uuuugh, fuck me already, Mel."

I slapped his ass. "Try again. What's my name?"

"Fuck me, Big Daddy."

"I can't hear you." I bit him again, hard.

"AAAAHH, FUCK ME, BIG DADDY!"

I rammed my cock in his ass, and he screamed my name. "FUCK, JAMEL! Aaah, fuck me, baby!"

I held both his hands above his head against the wall, and he allowed me to bury myself deep inside of him. I stroked my cock against his prostate, and he moaned out my name over and over again.

"Make me cum, baby. Fuck me harder, Mel, make me cum!"

I switched up my stroke, grabbed his waist and pounded into him over and over again. He hollered until cum flew out of his untouched penis upward onto the wall in front of him. I pulled him backward without pulling out, and we fell onto the loveseat by the door.

"Ride this dick, bitch," I commanded.

Connor laughed, then moved his waist back up against my abs as he rode to the head, then slid back down until my pubes scratched against his ass. He did this a few times, but then I held onto the back of his thighs pounding upward for a while until I got tired. I reached around him and stroked his dick hard again with one hand, reaching under his shirt and pinching his nipples with my other while he rode me by winding his waist against me in a circular way, and we moaned together.

I told him the same thing he told me, "Make me cum, baby. Fuck me harder and make me cum."

"I got you, Big Daddy. Hold on."

He leaned up and held onto my thighs, then bounced on my lap at warp speed. All I could do was hold onto his waist with one hand while stroking him with the other and let him impale himself on my cock. He moaned, "Ah! Ah! Ah!" loudly and didn't stop until my balls tightened, and I released cum deep inside of him. I stayed inside of him and jerked him off until he came again on my hands shortly afterward.

He fell backward against my chest, and I put my hand to his mouth to taste, making him moan in satisfaction. I wrapped my arms around him, and he held onto my arm. I kissed his neck and cheek a few times, then also leaned back. We sat this way still connected, with our eyes closed as our heartbeats slowed down. I love that we never needed words; it was enough for us to be one like this.

The doorbell rang. "Shit," I said, as we jumped up and scrambled to put back on our pants.

"Who the fuck is it?" Connor called out. Nobody answered.

I managed to get my pants up first and went to open the door. Ethan was standing there, leaning against the doorway. I had forgotten that I left him a voicemail.

"Yoooo shit," I found myself saying. "My bad about the frantic message. I'm okay now."

"Yeah, I know," he said amusingly. "I've been sitting in my car for about fifteen minutes, waiting for y'all to finish." He looked past me at Connor who was zipping up and said, "You're fucking loud. All your neighbors know Jamel's name."

I laughed loudly as Connor said, with a smile, "Shut the fuck up."

Ethan smirked and turned back to me. "I was in my office in a meeting when you called. I went to the Residence first, and neither of you were there so I came here. So, what do you want me to do? Handle it or nah?"

I sighed. "Nah. Connor's handling it. I trust him to." I turned around and looked at him, and his icy blue eyes sparkled with love for me.

Ethan shrugged. "Alright. Well since you don't need me, I'm gonna head—"

"No," Connor interrupted him. "Stay here. Jamel needs you. He needs a friend that he can talk shit to about his emotional, fag queen husband. But you know, y'all stubborn-ass, closed-mouth Scorpios don't know how to just say that; gotta be strong all the fucking time."

He grabbed his keys from the kitchen counter. "This emotional-ass Cancer is going to go find my emotionally sensitive but much wiser Pisces best friend, Lovie, and talk shit about mine."

Ethan laughed. "Okaaay. Maybe pick up that stubborn, arrogant, bull-headed Taurus husband of mine on the way. Since we're talking in terms of bad traits of our signs and all."

Connor smiled and patted his shoulder as he passed him to head out. But I pulled Connor back roughly and he allowed it, falling against me. I turned him around to face me.

"Thank you," I breathed on his lips. "I love you."

He kissed me softly. "Same."

CHAPTER 14

IF I'M HONEST

Jamel

The following weekend we were in my truck, headed to Dante's loft in downtown Providence. When I told Dante the idea of the threesome, first, he laughed and continued to laugh until I told him to forget it, then as I expected he jumped at the chance with a hearty, "Fuck, yeah! I get fucked by you *and* Connor, no strings attached? Hell fucking yeah!"

We agreed that it would be best to do it in Dante's space because we didn't want to bring our adventures into our home—our domesticated life as Connor calls it. We went over the rules before we left. But I added another one: no tongue-kissing. The one thing that continued to nag at me after our romp with Romy was watching them kiss. It dawned on me that the kissing was way too intimate, and he agreed.

Connor was excited all week, and it was infectious. By the end of the week, I was excited too, especially since I was turning forty the next day. It was going to be an epic night. But in the car on the drive over, Connor had a bit of nervous energy. He was quiet, in his head, and I could see it.

I asked him, "Are you okay?"

"Hmm?" he mumbled, as I pulled him from his thoughts. "Yeah, yeah. I'm good."

"What are you thinking about?"

He took a moment to answer. "When you were with Dante before, did you bottom for him?"

I smiled. "No. Dante is a full bottom with men. Only time he's on top is if he's with a woman." Then I was honest. "He wanted to though, switch with me. I told him no."

Connor looked at me. "Why?"

"You know why. It's a level of intimacy that I reserve."

"But you guys know each other. Been friends for over twenty-five years. And you do love each other on some level."

"Yes, but not on that level. I don't have any child-hood friends because of the way we moved around, except Dante. So, my love for him stems from that. Not from a romantic type of love for him."

He nodded and remained quiet. I asked him, "Are you having second thoughts? We don't have to do this if you don't want to."

"I want to," he said automatically. "You do too, right?"

"As long as I get to do it with you, yes."

"So, it doesn't matter who is in between?"

"Not really, no."

He smiled a little. "You'd do anything for me."

I smiled without looking at him. "You just figured that out?" He chuckled but didn't respond.

A long moment passed, then Connor said, "I changed my mind. You lead tonight."

He sounded a little far away when he said it. "Are you sure you're okay?" I asked again. "We can turn around right now if—"

"I'm fine." He reached over and took my hand. "Ready for another wild night?" He winked at me, making me laugh.

We made it to the waterfront property and took the elevator to his top floor loft, overlooking the Blackstone River. We held hands to his door and rang the bell.

Dante opened it dramatically in a pair of tight, knee-length leggings and a silk kimono robe opened to his bare chest. "Welcome to Hotel Dante! You may check out, but you just might never leave!"

We started laughing as we walked in and gave him hugs. "Wow," Connor exclaimed, and I knew why.

Dante's loft was immaculate. High ceilings, exposed brick walls and pipes painted black, long wood beams across the ceiling that matched the maple oak hardwood flooring. His white leather furniture looked like something out of a luxury magazine, and he even had a baby grand piano in the corner of the room, yet he didn't play.

Connor had never been in Dante's loft before because we didn't hang out with him. Through no fault of his or mine; we just lived very different lives and rarely got a chance to hang out, and that was before Connor came into my life. Dante was always on the move. Because he worked in computer programming, he could do his job from literally anywhere in the world, and he did. Dante would just get up and go, spending four months in France, come back to the states, then another six months in Ghana. He met beautiful people, had illustrious sex with them, and kept a blog of his escapades, changing names for anonymity. Even our night of drunken sex ended up there, thought it was written more like a short story between two friends who became passionate lovers in one night and had their memory erased in the morning. I appreciated his talented writing and discretion. Love and commitment were not things he had ever been interested in, although he kept his friend Blaine around. Even though Dante would never admit it, Blane was the one that Dante really cared about. But I always admired my friend's courage and his adventurous spirit.

Dante led us out to the sunroom that becomes a balcony in the summertime, but for now, all the windows are closed. He had a round table with drinks and a couple of joints on it. I knew Dante's drug of choice was coke, and I appreciated that I didn't have to ask him not to have it out, although I suspected he was already high. Other than smoking weed here and there, I didn't typically get high. Connor used to, mostly pills, but he also didn't get high anymore except once in a while with Donny. Connor's drug of choice was tequila anyway.

Connor took a joint but didn't sit. Instead, he walked to the large picture window, lit it, and looked out into the sunset. Dante and I sat down.

"So," Dante started, as he picked up a joint and lit it as well. "Are we going to pretend with small talk or get right to it?"

I smiled as I poured myself a glass of bourbon, and Connor chuckled. "You've never been one to mince words, Dante," Connor said, as he took a drag of his own joint. He handed it to me, and I took a small puff.

"Just like you, honey," Dante purred. "That's why Jamel loves us because we're so fucking honest and real to him. No apologies, no bullshit. We are who we are." He leaned back in his chair and smoked.

Connor glanced at me, then turned back to the sunset. "Yup. We are who we are."

I couldn't read him. I didn't like not being able to read him, especially when we were supposed to be in sync. It worried me, but I couldn't let that be known, not in front of Dante.

I tapped his hand and handed the joint back to him. "Well, you both know that I appreciate honesty above all else. That and being true to yourself. If everyone in the world would just do that, it would be a better place."

"And that's the one of the many things you've taught me, to be true to myself," said Dante.

I laughed. "I think that's the other way around."

"No, you are always true to yourself," Dante said. "You're just not open to everyone around because not everyone can handle your honesty. But for us that do, it makes us better people."

"He's right about that," Connor said. "Everyone around you is made better by your presence in their lives. Your honesty. It makes them want to live honestly too."

Connor turned around and looked into my eyes. We stared at each other as Dante got up and moved closer to him. He reached over and caressed Connor's perfect bottom. Connor broke eye contact with me and turned to my friend. Dante leaned into his neck and began to kiss him there. Connor closed his eyes, took another drag of the joint, then reached his hand out to me. I took it from him, took a small puff, then put it on the table to watch. I wasn't sure how I felt about it yet, seeing the two of them together like that. But when Dante lifted up his head and moved to kiss him, Connor casually turned his head; and that made me know everything was going to be alright.

Dante continued to kiss his neck while opening the buttons on his khakis. He went right to it: he dropped to his knees, pulled out Connor's cock, and covered it with his mouth. Connor put both hands on his head and said quietly, "Fffffuck."

I opened up my jeans and began to stroke myself. Connor saw and tapped Dante's head and said, "Go to him."

Dante looked up and smiled. He crawled over to me, and my first thought was, *I'm not high enough for this*. But then he took me in his mouth, and my eyes rolled to the back of my head. He sucked and rolled his tongue around the head of my cock, and it was phenomenal. I didn't remember his blow job being that great, but I also didn't remember much from that one time. He took me down inch by inch, but he couldn't make it all the way to the bottom before he gagged, then came back up. *Looks like he didn't remember much either.*

When he leaned up, I motioned toward Connor again, who was watching us, his dick standing straight out. Dante's smile let me know how badly he had been wanting to be fucked by Connor, probably all this time we've been together. And I was going to happily fuck him while he did it. He was going to break one of his own rules tonight just to be in the middle of us, so I guess we were all winning.

I sipped my drink and continued to smoke, leaving my cock exposed as Dante crawled back to Connor. He bobbed on him a few times, but then made his way up, pulling up his shirt and rubbing and kissing on his abs and chest as he stood up. He began kissing on Connor's neck again, sucked his earlobe, then kissed him behind his ear, and I knew that was my baby's spot. Connor began panting as Dante sucked on his ear and stroked his dick. I was high and drunk and loving every moment of watching my husband become undone.

Then Connor said breathlessly, "I love Aruba but."
Holy shit!

I didn't hesitate. I reached out and firmly grabbed Dante's wrist of the hand that was on Connor's genitals. Dante stopped and looked at me, but I was looking at Connor who was avoiding my eyes.

Dante asked, "What? You want to take it inside now?"

I stood up, pulling Dante's hand from my husband and stood in front of him, letting my jeans drop to the floor. I gently lifted my husband's head up so his eyes met mine. There was way too much uncertainty there.

Connor swallowed and said, "My stomach is bothering me. Something I ate ... I think."

I nodded. "Okay," I said casually. I turned to Dante. "We're gonna go. Another time, maybe."

Dante's face was stunned. "Whaaat?"

I shrugged as I pulled up my pants, my hard dick pulsating and Connor stuffed his own hard-on back in his pants. "Sorry, sweetheart. But I'm sure you'll be fine," I said to my friend.

"Did I do something wrong?" Dante asked, confused.

I touched his face and kissed his cheek. "Not at all, you did everything right. Thank you. I'll call you tomorrow."

I grabbed Connor's hand and kissed Dante's cheek again. Connor mumbled, "I'm really sorry," as I pulled him from the loft.

We walked to the car in silence, but when we got there, Connor held his hand out. "Let me drive. I was smoking a little, but you were drinking and smoking."

"Okay, baby." I handed him the keys to my truck.

Connor didn't get on the highway. He drove through the local streets of Providence, taking the long way home, keeping to the speed limit. After a couple of minutes, he said, "I love this truck. It's dependable and sturdy, just like you."

I laughed. "It's old, just like me."

He chuckled. "It's perfect, just like you."

I reached over and squeezed his leg. I meant to move it away, but he put his hand on mine, driving with his left hand instead of his right, and caressed my fingers.

After a stretch of silence, he said, "I'm sorry."

"For what? Stopping the train?" I shrugged. "Don't ever be sorry about that."

I waited because I knew he would tell me why. I didn't care that he ended it; I just wanted to make sure he was okay.

"I'm okay," Connor said, as if he was reading my thoughts. He sighed a big sigh. "I just... We just need to be in a good place when we do this. And after our fight the other day... Maybe I just need reassurance that we are."

"Connor, I told you, I didn't mean to say the things I said. Yes, you get emotional but it's what I love about you the most. How you care about—"

"Not that part. I am an immature, sensitive, emotional asshole when I want to be." He let a moment pass. "The part where you talked about me fucking Nate. Or letting him fuck me."

I sighed a big sigh too. "I trust you, Connor."

"I know that you trust me, but I also think somewhere deep down inside you expected me to be exactly who I've always been and ... stray."

And while I did have that deep fear, that was not what he needed to hear at the moment. Instead, I said, "Except it's not who you've always been. Who you are right now is who you've always been. That person who just wanted to be loved and to love back. The years you spent exploring your sexuality were just that, a period in your life that your grief drove you to, not to mention having it repressed all those years before

Vinnie died. I don't know one gay man that hasn't gone through that in some way, including me."

"But it's there, Mel," he implored. "If I'm honest… If I'm really honest… You didn't wake a sleeping dragon because it's always awake. I just don't let it loose. Which I guess is what normal people do, right? You see someone you're attracted to, but you don't act on it because what you have isn't worth losing. That desire isn't something I'm willing to gamble for the sake of my relationship. That's normal, right?"

"It is normal," I confirmed. "We all have a dragon in us that we can choose to let loose or keep it at bay, including me. It's not like I've never been attracted to someone else. But normal people also fuck up royally and act on those desires. If I'm honest, then yes, it is something that crosses my mind from time to time, you fucking up royally. But until Nate came along, it wasn't something that I actually worried about. But I saw you reject him. I watched you turn him down, not just for our marriage but for yourself. So, I trust you, Connor. The only thing I expect is for you to be honest, like right now. Just always be honest with me, and I promise you, we will get through anything."

He didn't respond at first, then said quietly, almost whispered, "I really want to ask you not to leave me."

"Pull over," I told him. Connor did.

I took off my seatbelt, turned to him in the car and moved closer. "Then ask me. Because I know you know it, but you need to hear the words. It's your love language. So, ask me every single day of your life. And every single day I will tell you."

I put his face in my hands and said, "Ask me."

Connor put his hands on mine, then reached across my shoulders. He looked at me with eyes as clear as the Caribbean Sea and said, "Don't leave me, okay? Even if I fuck up royally and fuck someone else without you. Even if I never want to have kids. Even if I yell at you and become a complete fucking ass- hole. Even if I scream at you to go. Don't ever leave me. Okay?"

I said automatically, "I'm never going to leave you, Connor. Ever."

We moved closer at the same time, nuzzled our nostrils together, and kissed softly a few times. Then we went home.

♥ ♥ ♥ CHAPTER 15 ♥ ♥ ♥

I Want To Do That

Connor

I didn't know why I was nervous to tell him; I was pretty sure he was going to be so happy and excited. But still, my stomach was in knots as we were sitting for dinner, just days after our twelfth anniversary.

"Sooooo, I want to talk with you about something," I started.

"Okay. You sound serious. What's up?" Jamel asked, as he was cutting through his flank steak.

"I was with Jack today at some shit dinner in Providence, and this sixteen-year-old kid who busses tables there came up to us. Apparently, he sees Jack for therapy. So he started talking and Jack tried to stop him, you know, confidentiality and all, but the kid was like, 'I don't give a shit; if you trust him then I do,' and he sat down, even though he was supposed to be working. He started telling Jack about how he's happy.

That for the first time in his life, he's making honor roll and taking care of himself. He's in a good place, even though he's got nowhere to go, and he plans to do what he has to do for money to survive when he ages out of the system, just so he can get a place for him and his little brother to go, who is four years younger and still in the system. Their mother is a drug addict, and they pretty much grew up in foster care, but they haven't been in the same home together since he was like ten. He's been in group homes most of the time because no one wants to take him in because he's gay, and he calls himself a reformed thief.

"So anyway, I got to talking with him and hearing about his life, and it's pretty fucked up. Right now, he's in some kinda independent living program, but he doesn't get to keep his money. He has to turn it over to the agency and that makes him mad, so he wants to leave before he turns eighteen and graduates. Jack and I were trying to convince him not to do that, because he's just going to end up turning tricks for money like he used to do and since he's been seeing Jack, he's been trying to go straight, for at least the last year. Anyway, he went back to work, and Jack and I left and we started talking and I was just like, Jamel and I should just take them, take them both in, but Jack said I couldn't do that because they're wards of the state so I don't know, I mean, I just thought that maybe you'd want to be foster parents and take these two kids in, so you know, they'd have someplace safe to live and sleep at night, and Luke could just work and go to school until he was ready to live on his own and take care of his brother, Angel."

I had been rambling for a little over a minute, and I watched Jamel slow down on his steak-cutting, put his knife and fork down, and look at me, giving me all his attention. He didn't say anything, and classic Jamel didn't give me a reaction on his face.

"You're gonna say something?" I asked.

"You want to become foster parents?" He turned the question back at me.

"Um … yeah, I guess. His story kinda reminds me of Nick's upbringing, with all the physical abuse and sexual abuse, and I don't want him to go through life not having at least one adult person he can count on. I mean he just seems like a good kid who got a really shitty hand in life so if we could help him and his brother… We have the room, and we could keep an eye on him, make sure he stays on the right track and in therapy… We could do it, right?"

Jamel nodded slowly. But I didn't know if that was a yes or an understanding. I got up and went to my bag in the front room and pulled out the envelope. I wanted to make sure I had all the paperwork to present to him, "doing the work" as he informed me last time we had a life-changing conversation.

When I sat back at the table, I handed it to him, saying, "I asked specifically which county and agency he is with, then I downloaded the application. We have to submit a bunch of stuff, do like twenty hours of training but we could be certified in, like, a month or so. I want to go back and tell him, but not until we're through the initial stages of it."

He took it from me but didn't open it. He put it on the table next to his plate, leaned back, and folded his hands.

I laughed nervously. "Okay, say something, Mel. I feel like we're having the healthcare-turned-marriage conversation all over again!"

Jamel smiled a little at that, then said, "Are you sure about this?"

"I mean yeah, I guess," I said again. "With fostering, at least the goal is for them to go back home, right? Or at least get settled so they can live on their own. Because I'm thinking older kids, not babies and toddlers. Like ten and up. I'm still not sold on actually adopting kids of my own, but helping kids get on their feet, give them a safe home for a while like we do with Freddie? Yeah. I could do that." I shrugged. Then said, "I want to do that."

He continued to stare at me with his unreadable gray eyes. "Mel, say something. Yay or nay?"

Jamel looked at me a bit more, then sighed. He returned to his fork and began eating again. "If that's what you want to do, Con, then okay," he said nonchalantly into his plate.

I watched him for a moment in disbelief, then said, "I'm going to kick your ass."

That made him laugh a big laugh. He grinned at me, and I grinned back. He got up and walked around the table, and I stood up, anticipating him. We hugged tightly first, then we kissed closed-mouth kisses a couple of times, then hugged again.

"Yay," he said softly.

And that's how we started.

EPILOGUE

Lucas and Angel were the first. The first couple of months were a bit rough, because we had to lay down some house rules, such as everyone goes to school, no matter what—that was for Angel, who wasn't used to going to school every day; and no randos for sex in the house—obviously that was for Luke. Jamel's "I'd rather them do it here than anywhere else" mindset went out the door when he saw the type of randos he was bringing home. Luke was used to doing what he wanted, didn't like rules, and especially didn't trust adults. He ran away with his brother a month in but came back three days later and said that Angel begged him to come back, saying it was the safest place he had been in a while. The agency asked if we wanted them moved after they came back, and we both said absolutely not. They were already ours.

When Luke was eighteen and Angel was fourteen, we officially adopted them, despite Luke already being an adult. After Luke graduated high school, Jamel took him on as an electrician apprentice and by the time he was twenty, he was able to take a test to become a certified electrician and do honest work, making real money. By the time he was twenty-three, Luke wanted to live on his own so Ethan gave him an apartment in East Greenwich, ten minutes from the house. Angel, who was nineteen at the time and working with Jamel in the family construction business, moved in with Luke to give us the room and space to foster more children. Our sons still come over almost daily, and especially for Sunday dinner every week.

We kept fostering, seeking out LGBTQ teens that were abused, abandoned, and left in the system. Most did go home, like Adam, a trans boy who we helped form relationships with other members of his family after his parents kicked him out. He lives in DC with his cousin now and is doing pretty well for himself. Others stayed until they were able to stand on their own two feet, get a job, get their own place. If they weren't in school after eighteen, we didn't get a subsidy for them but we wanted them to stay anyway until they felt like they could move on.

Fiona stayed the longest. If she wanted to be adopted, we would have. But she made it clear she never wanted that, that she would always be a Robinson, her late father's only daughter. She just wanted a home where she wasn't going to be molested or raped at night. We took her in at fourteen, and she lived with us until she was twenty-five, then she met a guy and decided to move in with him, which we weren't happy about. But she is okay. She calls us her dads and comes over for Sunday dinner too.

The youngest we ended up taking in was a sibling group of four between the ages of five and thirteen. That was probably the closest I ever came to wanting to adopt young children. But a rich, childless couple that Mary Kate and Dennis met during their own adoption journey wanted them after finding them on the Adopt US Kids website and meeting them in person at our house. They were going to have better, fuller lives with them so we let them go, but stayed in contact with them and became their uncles. We fostered over twenty children and raised three as our own, not including Freddie, who tells everyone he was our first kid. And really, he's not wrong.

Five years after my father died, I wrote a book about my life. I gave a forward dedicating it to my mother, "the strongest woman I've ever known," and apologized to anyone who would be hurt by this, but I needed to finally speak my truth. I warned my sisters and my mom, Afia, Mina, Winter, and especially Bethany, Vinnie's widow, that it was all going to come out. They all said to me, in one way or another, "Good" and "It's about time." Bethany sent me pictures of Vinnie as a kid to add to the book, so I dedicated a whole chapter in my book to his life. Matty tried to sue me for defamation, but since my mother and sisters backed me up, he didn't have a leg to stand on.

I named it *The Truth About Silence: Finally Freeing My Voice and Living My Truth*. Jamel was right; I needed to free my voice, not just for myself but for others. Sure

I got the occasional nasty, "You're going to burn in hell" emails, but the love and support I got from strangers was overwhelming: men who were physically abused growing up; straight and gay men who went through periods of sexual exploration; military men who also fell in love during the DADT era and had to lie about who they were to be able to continue to serve. They all thanked me for my raw honesty and openness. I didn't change any names, so even Lex showed up in there, but only as Lex, not his full name, just like Romy. The only secret I kept was my mother's secret of the day my father died. I never even told Jamel; that will go with me to my grave.

A year after the book was published, Leo Barrone, at age twenty-one, showed up unannounced at my door. He was in his Marines uniform so when I opened it, I almost fainted and the tears started falling out before I could stop them. He was a splitting image of Vinnie, only his hair was a little blonder and his eyes were blue. Like if Vinnie and I had a baby, that's what he would look like. He, like everyone else, did not know his father was gay. His mother sat him down and told him, then gave him the book to read when it came out. He went through a lot of emotions but ended up grateful for his story and legacy coming out. Vinnie's Vet Buddies is his father's legacy. Also with his mother's permission, he gave me Vinnie's flag, folded and encased, with a note that said she should have sent it to me a long time ago; that it always belonged to me as Vinnie's true love.

We never did go back and have a threesome with Dante. But every couple of years, Jamel and I got adventurous and invited a third with us, no one we knew. I don't know why it kept our marriage healthy, but it did. It made us communicate better and be honest in our feelings in ways we haven't done before. And Jamel, true to his word and love for me, grew old with me. His love for me is infinite and my love for him is open, no longer hidden.

BOOK CLUB QUESTIONS

♥ • ♥ • ♥ **BOOK CLUB QUESTIONS** ♥ • ♥ • ♥

1) The first three books of the series were Connor's perspective alone. How did it feel to have Jamel's internal thoughts and feelings about Connor in the last two books?

2) Tyrell and Connor continue to have a contentious relationship a decade later. Why do you think that is? Is there anything that Connor could do to fix it? Did the ending change things for Ty?

3) What are your thoughts around ethically non-monogamous relationships?

4) Describe the relationship between Jamel and the Four Musketeers, especially with Freddie, and the implications for Jamel's desire to raise children.

5) How did you feel about the relationship between Jamel and Katherine McIntyre? How does it

compare to the relationship between Connor and Jamel's mother, Mama Denita?

6) 2020 was significant for Jamel and Connor. What stood out to you the most: how they faired through the global pandemic mentally, emotionally, and financially? Connor and Jamel raising Freddie? The impact of the death of George Floyd on Jamel? Jack and Ethan's family becoming closer to Jamel and Connor's family?

7) In the week of Owen McIntyre's death and leading to his funeral, several things happened, including Afia's acknowledging the extent of Owen's racism toward her; Jamel and Connor's dog passing away; Nate's true intentions of befriending Connor; Owen's continued abuse of his wife up to the day of his passing; and Connor having a panic attack right before the wedding. What were your thoughts about Connor's handling of each situation? Of Jamel's handling the situation?

8) Debate the circumstances of Owen McIntyre's death. Did Katherine kill her husband by not getting him medical treatment?

9) Was Connor justified in the way he handled Matthew at the repass?

10) How did you feel about Jamel's outburst to Connor? Was it unnecessary or well overdue?

11) After years of pushback, Connor decided for them to become foster parents and eventually adopt

children. Did he do it for Jamel, for their relation-ship, or for himself?

12) How has Connor changed throughout the series? How has Jamel?

13) Did you feel a sense of closure for them by the end of the epilogue? A happily ever after? Why or why not?

14) If the series were made into a movie or series, who would you want to play each of the lead characters?

♥ ♥ ♥ AUTHOR BIO ♥ ♥ ♥

Wife, mother, partner, daughter, sister, friend, social worker, life skills coach, and part-time erotic romance novelist, Eskay Kabba finds the complexity of human nature and her characters reflect the notion that no one is all good or all bad, but we are all just trying to find love in hard places. Eskay pens erotic romance novels that celebrates the LGBTQ community, people of color, and interracial relationships. When not writing about the throes of passion, Eskay finds joy in spending time with her family and loved ones, reading dystopia and fantasy series, and binging popular shows from a streaming app. Eskay. Kabba@gmail.com

MORE BOOKS FROM
4 HORSEMEN PUBLICATIONS

LGBT EROTICA

DOMINIC N. ASHEN
Steel & Thunder
Storms & Sacrifice
Secrets & Spires
Arenas & Monsters
My Three Orc Dads: a Novella

Lookin in All the Wrong Places
What Makes Me a Whore?
A Breach in Confidentiality
Back Door Pass
My European Adventure
An Unexpected Affair
Finding True Love

ESKAY KABBA
Hidden Love
Not So Hidden
Signs of Affection
Deeply Devoted to Him

LEO SPARX
Before Alexander
Claiming Alexander
Taming Alexander
Saving Alexander
The Case of Armando

GRAYSON ACE
How I Got Here
First Year Out of the Closet
You're Only a Top?
You're Only a Bottom?
I Think I'm a Serial Swiper

ROBERT LEWIS
Someone to Love
Someone to Come Home To

LGBT ROMANCE

ESKAY KABBA
Hidden Love
Not So Hidden
Signs of Affection
Deeply Devoted to Him

Mikaél's Moment: Type 6
Stephan's Resurgence: Type 5
Anastasia's Arrival: Type 6

STORMIE SKYES
Check Yes, No, or Maybe

LUCAS LAMONT
Roman's Reckoning: Type 6

DISCOVER MORE AT
4HORSEMENPUBLICATIONS.COM